Praise for Christine Cochrane an.

'My third winner was 'Shifting sa... ...y Christine Cochrane, which is set in South Uist and Benbecula, where wild weather and the sea govern the characters' movements. This story has the dream-like intensity of myth. The title of this story really works, both literally and metaphorically.'
– *Jane Rogers, Mslexia short story competition 2014*

'An impressive sense of place, and language which is alive and supple.'
– *Nicky Harlow*

'Scotland and the Western Isles are brought alive for the reader.'
– *Hilary K. Brown, Edition Narrenflug, Kiel.*

'A fascinating new voice from Scotland.'
– *Gabriele Haefs*

For my family and friends

Shifting Sands

❧

Tales of transience and transformation

❧

Christine Cochrane

Published in 2015 with the help of:
Lumphanan Press
Roddenbrae, Lumphanan,
Aberdeenshire, AB31 4RN

www.lumphananpress.co.uk

Cover photograph by Iain Redbrook: Traigh Mhor, Isle of Tiree

Printed and bound by:
Imprint Digital, Upton Pyne, Devon, UK.

ISBN: 978-0-9927468-5-8

Contents

Shifting sands

❧

On the western shore of the island there is no shelter. There is no land between here and America and, when the westerlies blow, the villagers call the cattle in and lie low in the squat stone-built crofts on the lee side of the church. The breakers roar on the white beach like muffled thunder.

Donald leaves his plot on the machair in the late afternoon and heads home, for he knows from the purple line on the horizon that a storm is coming. Cloud is swirling on Beinn Mhor as he follows the track to the church of Howmore.

It is then that he hears the baby's cry.

His collie, Luath, growls and sniffs the air, the hairs on the back of his neck rising. There is a movement by the church door, and then Donald sees the figure hunched on the step, clutching her ankle. The girl pulls a rough plaid over her thin shoulders and looks up at him. She can't be more than eighteen. Her long, fair hair is unkempt, sticky with the salt of the sea, and her eyes turn towards the baby's cries, now more distant.

'Can I help?' Donald speaks softly. He has never seen the girl before. She is not from this island.

Her grey eyes are piercing. Donald feels uncomfortable,

knowing she is taking in the roughness of his hands, his weathered face, his windblown hair.

'My baby…'

Tears fill her eyes as she tries to stand.

'Your baby?'

'I fought… but she was snatched away… and my ankle…'

She winces as she puts weight on her foot. Donald touches her shoulder gently.

'We had better be taking you somewhere warm,' he says.

A bubbling stockpot hangs over the peat fire in the blackhouse, filling the air with a smoky, savoury tang. Four children sit in height order on the edge of the box bed, their wide eyes directed towards Eilidh, for that is her name. Luath growls in the shadows.

'Are you a fairy?' asks Mhairi. She is five years old and never shy.

Eilidh cradles the bowl of broth.

'No… I don't think so…'

'Let her be, child. Can't you see that she is tired? We will let her rest, and then maybe she can tell us more,' says Donald.

'And who on earth was it that took your child? We must be knowing this if we are to help.' It is the voice of Donald's wife, Morag.

'I cannot say. I ran and ran. Somehow I tripped… and in the struggle she took her…'

'It was a woman?'

Eilidh swallows, then nods. 'I must go…'

Donald restrains her. He looks at Morag. He looks at his

children, who seem drawn to the visitor. He takes his coat from the hook by the door.

'You rest.' He nods at Eilidh. 'I'll do what I can.'

'Be careful!' Morag cries. The flames leap in the grate as the door slams. The rain lashes on the window and the wind sings like distant organ pipes in the hollow of the chimney.

Catriona staggers along in the fading light of early evening, buffeted by the gusts from the west. The track runs over moorland, past Loch Bi where the sad cries of geese are carried on the wind. She walks with purpose, for she knows that she and the baby in her arms must cross South Ford, the shifting sands between South Uist and Benbecula, before high tide. At the top of the rise by Rhuabal she looks back briefly and, imagining she can see a hint of a movement by the crofts at Geirinis, she quickens her pace. Benbecula. She says the name under her breath and half jogs to the rhythm of it. She does not look back.

Rounding the final twist in the road, she sees the waves rippling high on the beach and wonders if she is too late. But then in the dusk she can make out the dark spokes of two huge wheels and the tossing heads of horses. They call it the machine, the trap with two horses that plies the Ford under the skilled eye of Seamus.

'Is it yourself, Seamus?' she cries into the gloom.

'Make haste, the tide is coming in fast!'

Seamus holds out a hand to help her and, panting with the strain of it, Catriona hauls herself and the baby up into the trap beside a thin-lipped woman and her young daughter, both wrapped in tweed against the weather. The daughter eyes the lapping waves in terror.

'Will we make it?' she cries, leaning over the side of the trap.

'Aye, that we will, lass. Now you hold on tight.'

Seamus grips the reins and mutters calming words to the horses. The trap creaks and, as they pull away, there is a cry in the darkness. A man leaps across the sand and lurches into the empty seat, and Catriona sees that he fixes his eye on her.

Morag sits by the fire as the storm roars, thinking of Donald who has always been there and who is now absent. She thinks of how he was clever and sat at the back of the schoolroom by the map of The World, and how she would ask him for help with the arithmetic and the verbs. The clock ticks, and in the embers of the fire she sees them older now, courting. She hears the music of village ceilidhs, where they danced on the long, white nights to Ruaraidh's fiddle. Her eyes turn to the children, asleep with Eilidh beside them, and she thinks of the good father he is.

Through the evening Eilidh has told tales of an island she does not name. And when the children were fretful, she sang to them, a lullaby in a strange key. And instantly they were soothed.

Morag alone is awake.

Donald watches Seamus pick out the safe channels. The horses zigzag warily across the sands, water lapping at their fetlocks. The lights of Creagorry blink like a row of small lighthouses through the rain, and the wind sings round Donald's ears. He swallows, turning to the woman he knows he must confront.

Her dark hair is tinged with grey, and she looks down at the baby so that he cannot see her expression. With a wry smile, he sees how the baby sleeps through it all. When to speak, that is the question, for the second woman, who says her name is Alanna, fixes him with her gaze. How foolish to think that he could simply take the baby! The trap creaks and groans, listing to precarious angles.

Suddenly there is a rumble, a rushing of water and a terrified whinnying, loud and shrill. One of the horses has stumbled, losing its footing in the eddying current. Donald grips the seat as the broad backs of the horses rear up before him and the trap begins to rock and tilt.

'Is it not safer to be going back?' the dark-haired woman cries, clutching the baby to her breast.

Seamus wrestles to regain control. They are half way across.

'Yell your lungs out! There can be no turning back!' Seamus cries. 'Aonghuis Beag may be there with his boat in Creagorry, God help us!'

The trap rocks like a boat on the Minch. Water seeps through the floor planks, gurgling round their feet.

'Swim!' yells Seamus.

Donald feels icy needles around him. His feet reach out for the sandy bottom, but there is nothing there. Seamus reaches for Alanna and her daughter, and in a twist of fate Donald knows it is he who must help the baby thief. He longs for the warmth of the blackhouse that was his father's home and his grandfather's, on the special land that is his, with the harebells and campions blooming on the machair in summer. He hears the croaking of corncrakes and the buzzing of bees in the orchids, and he knows that when the sun shines there is no more beautiful place on earth. He longs for Morag, ladling out warm soup, and reflects on her face and her hands that work so hard, chapped by the work on the crops in the rain and the cold, coated in oats from the baking. Then Donald gulps and chokes, realising the hands he can see are his own, floundering in the water, white and swollen.

Donald tries to grab the baby thief, but can only clutch at her tweed jacket, heavy with water. Struggling to hold the weight of her and the baby, he loses sight of the guiding lights on shore. His legs feel weak, his lungs small. He sees himself in the schoolyard, the others in the class towering over him. You can do the spelling, and the arithmetic, and the Latin, but you will never make the shinty team, the schoolmaster said. Nor are you a swimmer, and that is not a good thing in this wet and windy island of ours. Donald feels anger at the schoolmaster course through his veins, forcing him to keep afloat. Then the clouds part, and in a thin shaft of moonlight he sees a rowing boat head towards them. A voice cries out 'Catriona!'

In the cottage at Creagorry, Catriona sits by the fire. She has changed into dry clothes and has offered Donald garments belonging to her husband, Aonghuis Beag.

'You must stay with us tonight,' she says to Donald. 'There can be no going back until the morning.'

'Thank you,' he whispers.

'It is I who must thank you,' she says. 'You saved me. You saved my child.'

In the flickering firelight, she watches Donald. He has

stopped shivering now, and he stares at her for a long time, his brow furrowed.

'She said she was the mother,' he says at length.

'Who? I don't understand.'

'The girl who came to our croft. Thin, with piercing grey eyes.'

'You must see that this is my child, Donald! And many years it was that we waited for her, Aonghuis and I.'

Catriona hugs the child to her.

'Then who is she?' Donald asks.

The door bursts open, and Aonghuis comes into the dimly lit room.

'We have got them,' he says. 'With the help of Niall at the harbour. Both horses back on shore, and Alanna and her child safe.'

'Thank the Lord,' Donald says. 'But…'

Catriona watches Donald twisting his hands. Then he stands up and paces the room.

'Who is this girl? The girl that took the baby?'

Catriona knows what she must tell him.

'It was today that I, too, asked this question. A girl as you describe came to the village yesterday and played with the children on the beach. She asked to hold our young one, and she sang to her.'

'Aye, and a strange melody it was, in a key I could not name. I have never heard the like,' Aonghuis says.

'And this morning I had the baby with me at the plot. I curse myself, for I had laid her down while I was digging, and in a moment she was gone in the arms of this girl who ran fast as a deer.' Catriona hugs the child to her. 'And I followed her, as you must know, but I did not get over until the next crossing. If she had not stopped to rest near Howmore I would not have caught up.'

Donald jumps to the door. 'My wife, my children…'

'There can be no going back until the daylight and the turning of the tide,' says Aonghuis. 'You must stay with us.'

Catriona sleeps fitfully through the night, holding the baby to her heart. She knows that Donald is awake.

Morag takes the cattle down to the pasture by the sea. In the morning sunlight, in the air clear and rainwashed, she sees two dark specks on the white beach of Howmore. One is Eilidh, who is no longer lame. The other is Mhairi, who plays with pebbles where the sea shines turquoise.

Morag takes in the beauty of it and breathes deeply. Donald will return with the baby; he will come soon. Turning from the figures on the shore, she heads back to the croft. Buds are appearing, and in a month, when the flowers are in full bloom, their land will hold all the colours of the rainbow.

Morag sees the moving figure on the road by the schoolhouse. She knows it is Donald, but there is a firmness in his step that was not there before.

Donald embraces her quickly.

'Did you not find the child? Donald, what has happened?'

'Where is she?' Donald asks, taking her by the shoulders, looking into her eyes with a fire that surprises her. She steps back.

'Where is Eilidh? You must tell me.'

'On the beach, with Mhairi. She is so good with the children, Donald. You must come and see…'

Donald takes her hand, pulling her with him.

They run to the beach, but the white sands are empty.

Cross words

✧

Jim eased himself into the day with a cup of strong coffee. From his lounger, he watched the sun gradually light up the terraces of orange groves and almond trees that led down to the coast at Nerja. The small dot on the dusty track got bigger; Fran had been up since seven and was heading back from her morning power walk. In a minute he'd hear the neighbours' dogs barking behind the iron gates as she passed. Jim didn't mind them quite as much later in the day, after he'd had a glass of wine or two, but he wished they'd have a bit more respect before ten.

He heard the door open. Her footsteps echoed in the tiled hallway. Then there was silence.

'Jim, will you come and look at this!' Fran's voice was insistent. 'Your grandchild's on Facebook!'

'My grandchild hasn't been born!' Jim muttered. He picked up the *Telegraph* and headed indoors.

Fran had the laptop open on the table. Her face glowed; she was wearing a white T-shirt that complemented her tan.

'I assure you, Jim, our grandchild is here. As a scan,' she added. 'Ally's made it her profile picture. Nice scan, but I do wonder if that's going a bit far...'

'Good God! You mean the fruit of my daughter's womb is in the public domain?'

Fran shrugged and clicked "Like". 'That's the way they do it these days, Jim.'

'But, I'd like to have seen it myself first. Privately, you know. Just the two of us.' Jim shook his head and eased himself on to the sofa. He adjusted his position to make the waistband of his shorts more comfortable. All his trousers seemed too tight these days.

'I know what you mean, but…' Fran puckered her lips and pushed her reading glasses onto the top of her head.

Jim liked the blonde highlights she'd had done recently.

'Don't take it so seriously, Jim,' she added, patting his hand. 'Have you finished the crossword, yet?'

'Only four to get.'

They got the *Telegraph* once a week. Jim sniffed the paper, hoping Fran wouldn't notice. The inky smell of newsprint transported him back to the *Epsom Guardian* and the pub lunches on Fridays with Mike. Retirement meant he didn't have anything to report on, which he found unsettling.

'Poisonous in one country for heady feeling.' Jim scratched his head and frowned.

'How many letters?'

'Twelve. Fourth one's an "o", second last one's an "o" too.'

'No consonants? They make it easier.'

Jim smiled. Fran, the teacher. She had always been good with words. She could speak Spanish too. She was much better at it than he was. In fact, she could multi-task: she did pilates in Spanish. You had to make an effort with retirement, she said.

He glanced over at CD Two of the Michel Thomas Spanish Course and made a mental note to do some later.

'I'll think about it while I whizz up some cupcakes for the book club,' Fran said, snapping the laptop shut. It was the latest Dell, in bright pink. 'It probably ends in "tion" though…'

Jim glanced at his watch. Two hours until it was a respectable time to open the wine. He settled down with the crossword.

'Intoxication!' Fran shouted from the kitchen.

'That's it,' said Jim, filling in one across. 'Three to go.'

Mike would have got that one, he thought. He was good at prompting. Didn't just shout the answer out. Jim felt a pang for the *Running Horses* with its sticky copper-topped tables and the stale smell of beer-drenched towelling mats on the bar.

❦

'Can't get three down. Warbled a backward tune for foreign drink. Five letters.' Jim tossed the clue over to Mike.

'Should be easy. Warbled… trilled… sang…'

'Got an 's' and a 'g' in it, so that could fit. Sang… sangria!' Jim smiled and swigged his pint.

'Plenty of that where you're heading, mate.' Des, the barman, nodded over to them, polishing some already clean glasses. 'Can't be bad. Taking the wife, then?' He grinned.

'Well… she organised it really.'

'Can't believe how quickly it all came together for you,' Mike said.

'The cottage was always going to sell. Lovely garden… too much work though.'

'Blimey! Bet you're looking forward to a bit of a relax. You been working on that paper a month of Sundays. How long's it been, mate?' Des selected an empty glass for himself.

'Started on the *Guardian*... the *Epsom Guardian*... when I was twenty-three. Forty years of news.' Jim stared into space. 'Reporting, the paper, it's what I've always done... worked with words.'

'So where is it exactly?' Mike interrupted Jim's reverie.

'Place called Cómpeta, up in the hills. About fifteen miles from the coast, east of Málaga. I wanted to be nearer the sea, then Fran said we got more house for our money up there. Away from the rowdiness of the coastal strip, that's what she said.'

'Oh, I love the coastal strip, me.' Des was pulling himself a pint. 'Be out there like a shot. Get down them bars. Cheers Jim!' He raised his glass. 'Have fun, mate!'

'Here's to your new life, lucky Jim!' Mike put down the crossword and clinked his glass against Jim's.

❧

'So there we were, Jim and I, squelching through some muddy lane down by Dorking, saying "can't take much more of this wet" when I suddenly thought – we don't have to do this!' Fran paused to pull up her hood while Jenny opened the field gate. The path wound on over the Downs towards Juniper Hill. Overhead, a plane droned on its descent into Gatwick. It was raining quite hard now, but Fran and Jenny had a rule to go out for their ladies' walk day whatever the weather.

'You're so right, Fran! You don't have to do this! You can have sun every day. What's not to like? Do they have a pilates class, though?' Jenny adjusted the straps on her walking poles.

'Yes, checked that. Body Control.'

'You deserve some "you" time. You really do. All those years working your socks off for Dorking High. And of course, you speak a bit of Spanish. You'll miss Ally though. And Magnus.'

'Ally was all for it. She and Magnus will come and stay, of course. Quick hop from Gatwick. Ideal holiday for them, really. They've got a huge mortgage and, well, you know… hoping to start a family soon…'

'Can we come too?'

Fran nodded and laughed. They walked on into the rain.

❧

A soft breeze rose in the early evening, blowing the scent of thyme and rosemary onto the terrace. Jim was reluctant to go indoors but remembered his date with Michel Thomas.

The two-storey villa on the edge of town was light and airy with its terracotta floor tiles and whitewashed walls but, even with all their familiar furniture and photos about, Jim couldn't escape the notion that it seemed like a holiday house. Fran had tried to make up for its distance from the sea by placing binoculars on the windowsill.

Heading for the CD player by the fireplace, he brushed against his old guitar. On impulse, he twanged the strings playfully. Dust particles floated into the air. And suddenly he was back in his attic room at university, singing something about being lonely in the streets of London. Jim coughed, then slotted the Michel Thomas Spanish CD into the player.

Michel built things up gradually. You didn't need to write anything down. Jim simply had to translate the sentences into Spanish in the gap provided.

'What do you have?'

'Qué tiene?'

'What impression do you have?'

'Qué impresión tiene?'

'The political situation.'

'La situación política.'

'What impression do you have of the political and economic situation?'

'I can't say that!'

'What?' Fran put her head round the door.

'I can't open a conversation with any Spaniard about the political and economic situation!'

'Well, it got us this house. So many Brits wanting to sell up. Not us, though. Living the dream.' Fran put an arm round Jim and held out the iPad. 'Check out the baby bump.'

Jim looked at his daughter's belly. The stripes of Ally's jumper, distorted by the small bulge beneath, made his eyes go funny.

'What the—?' Jim squinted at the photo. 'Can everyone see this?'

'Well, all her Facebook friends. Anyway, it's coming along, isn't it? Fran beamed. 'I wonder if they're thinking of names. Olivia, now that's a nice one for a girl. And for a boy... not sure. What do you think?'

'I think... I wish we lived closer.'

'But Jim, we're loving it. It's warm, for heaven's sake. Trouble with you is, you need to do more. You're a bit *mañana* with that Spanish. Join a choir! Do an OU course! You always said you wanted to write fiction.'

'And you… you're either out gallivanting or welded to that bloody iPad.' Jim was surprised at the irritation that welled up. He steadied himself on the back of the chair as he stood up. 'For God's sake, Fran, I just thought… we'd do more things together. Is that too much to ask?'

'Well, let's talk about it!' Fran pursed her lips.

'I can't talk, because you're always off somewhere. If it's not cupcakes for Susanna's book club, it's Spanish pilates or tennis or…'

'I'm keeping mind and body fit, Jim. Making the most of my retirement. Which is more than you are!'

'I'm going out! I need some air.' Jim's heart was hammering as he slammed the heavy wooden door behind him. Fearing for a moment that it might lead to a heart attack, he sat down on a bench by the roadside, thinking of Fran with the iPad, hard and cold in her hand. He could see her face, her wide-eyed stare. He had silenced her.

⁊

The air vibrated with the sound of flamenco. Jim followed the cobbled lane that zigzagged down towards the central square and found himself outside *Fernando's*. Pushing his way through the early evening crowds, he entered the bar. A young man with a moustache sat on a low stool, slapping a guitar, while a dark-haired girl trilled and warbled in a deep alto voice. Something about her made Jim think of Fran in their student days, laughing and vibrant. Fernando's wife lifted their young daughter up into her arms, laughing.

Fernando was wiping down the counter, looking dapper in his black apron.

'Una cerveza por favor.' Jim pointed to the beer just to make sure.

'Si, señor Jim. Cómo estás?'

So Fernando knew his name. Fran usually did the talking.

'Solo, señor Jim?' Fernando enquired.

'Si ... er ... solo. Fran ... at home ... en casa.' His confidence rose with the first gulp of San Miguel. 'Muy bien, la cerveza,' he added.

'Español! Muy bien!' Fernando probed further. 'Que impresión tiene de la musica?'

'La musica ... muy bien! La impresión ... muy bien!'

'Tiene una guitarra?' Fernando mimed guitar-playing, pointing at Jim.

'Si ... si, Fernando. I have ... tengo ... una guitarra!'

❦

Fran paced the room, holding the iPad. She had it on Skype.

'Aw, he'll get over it, Mum. Just, like, give him time.'

'I just wish he'd do more, Ally. I've been up for two hours before he even stirs. Sometimes he's just... sitting. Keen on his wine, though. Getting nowhere with the Spanish. And I mean, I don't get it. He's good with words.'

'Yeah, well, that's Dad.'

'Still doing his crosswords, of course. Gets the *Telegraph* once a week for a treat. I was just thinking about his guitar the other day. Because that's how we met, of course... the folk club...'

'Aw, cut the hippy stuff, Mum. He'll get over it, honest. It's a guy thing. Can you sit down? Picture's breaking up.'

'The thing is, Ally, I'm just not sure he's going to be OK with this...'

ↄ

Rodriguez, the flamenco player, guided Jim's awkward hand into position on the frets of the guitar and watched him strum a chord.

'Si! Si! Señor Jim! Magnifico!'

'Una situación magnifico!'

'Magnifica,' Rodriguez corrected. He guided Jim's hand into a different position, and demonstrated the strumming technique.

Fernando was impressed. He reached for a leaflet from the bar. 'Rodriguez, he teach Wednesday. Is easy. La musica es internacional! Una situación muy bien!'

Jim studied the leaflet.

Una situación magnifica; he matched the rhythm of the sentence to his homeward steps.

ↄ

Up at the villa, away from the town centre, Jim could see the stars shine bright in the night sky above the silhouetted

Almijarra foothills. In the distance the snake of orange lights wound along the coast, and beyond that was the darkness of the Mediterranean, and Africa. He felt that anything was possible.

Jim pushed open the front door and stopped suddenly in the darkness of the hall. There were voices in the lounge.

'He'll be OK, Mum. Honest. Anyway… I'm, like, so excited. I can't wait. I want to feel the baby move… that'll be soon, won't it?'

'Oh, yes. I remember how it was with you.' Fran's voice was quiet, gentle. 'There I was at the kitchen window in Mickleham, looking out on the apple blossom…'

'Aw, Mum… And me and Magnus have got the first antenatal class next week. He's gonna be really hands on. And his mum was like, yeah, I'll have plenty time to help now I'm retired.'

There was silence, then Ally's voice came again. 'Mum?'

'That's lovely, darling.' Fran paused.

'Mum? Are you all right, Mum?'

'I remember first holding you,' Fran said. 'There was a bird singing by the window.'

'Aw, cheers Mum. You're sentimental tonight.'

'I was just thinking about your father again, that's all. Not often we have cross words. You'll maybe come for Christmas?'

'Christmas? Definitely. Bye Mum. Miss ya. Gotta go.'

Fran's face was in shadow. She jumped when Jim spoke.

'I'm sorry, love.' He seemed hesitant.

'Jim… Jim… I want to go home.' She paused, and placed the iPad on the table. 'I want to hold the baby.'

Jim laid the flamenco leaflet beside the iPad. 'I know, love, but I think… I think… we'll be OK. Just taking me, taking us, a bit of time. You're always so busy and…'

Jim watched Fran pick up the leaflet.

She nodded, then sidled a little closer towards him. 'Finish the crossword together, Jim?'

Ships that pass

❧

The events of 'Ships that pass' are mainly fictional but are inspired by fragments of a diary written by Mary McNicol, Glasgow, 1905.

Ships that pass in the night, and speak each other in passing,
Only a signal shown and a distant voice in the darkness;
So on the ocean of life, we pass and speak one another,
Only a look and a voice, then darkness again and a silence.

– Longfellow

Someone had made a circle of stones in the sand. Although it was nearly eleven o'clock at night, that magical white light of midsummer still bathed the island. Robert Campbell had locked the dark green door of the cottage and walked with his mother to her favourite place, Tangasdale Bay. After the turmoil of packing everything up, they both needed the calm it offered. From their usual bench by the shore, Robert watched their two shadows grow long and thin on the cropped grass while they listened to the munching sheep. The honey scent of clover mingled with the salt of the sea, and they sat in silent companionship watching the sun slip down towards the horizon.

Robert had fond memories of his island childhood. His father had been the island doctor in Castlebay for thirty-five years, and Robert thought of how his parents used to stand with him at the window of Calagorm, the doctor's house, and point out Vatersay and the islands that stretched south like a necklace towards the jewel of steep-cliffed Mingulay. Beyond that, the lonely lighthouse of Berneray flashed in the night at passing ships, marking the last outpost of the island chain. Robert, now resident in Helensburgh, returned every summer with his wife Anne and the children. They would walk on the white beaches and take the boat out to fish in the bay, and he would show them secret places that only he knew.

This summer, however, was tinged with sadness, as he had come alone to the island to help his mother pack.

'Once your father saw the island practice there was nowhere else he wanted to be. Between patients he could watch the ships.' His mother's words drifted gently on the light breeze. She liked to speak of his father. Robert listened to her refined Glasgow accent, every consonant clear.

The doctor had never thought of retiring from his work. He had died, unexpectedly, of a heart attack after one of his evening surgeries. Robert's mother had moved out of the doctor's house to make way for the next incumbent and, for the last five years, had lived in Tangasdale Cottage, surrounded by possessions and memories. But the winters were long and dark, and she had finally decided that it would be sensible to come to Helensburgh to live with Robert and his family.

'My heart is here in Barra, but I'm not getting any younger,' she'd say.

She seemed strong and well, as far as Robert could tell. She still liked to walk on the beach and the hills. But there was no doubt that she missed his father.

'We'll come back for holidays. Every summer.' Robert patted her thin hand. Her skin was brown and wrinkled from the sun. 'And you can watch the ships from our house in Helensburgh.'

'That's true. There's no turning back the decision now,

Robert. After all you've done for me on the house. And after all the packing and sorting!'

Robert had done well in his business and owned a handsome villa up on the hill at Helensburgh. They had converted part of the house into a flat for her. You could see the Clyde from its bay windows; he knew his mother would not have consented to go had it not been for that view to the south west.

Today had been a day of discoveries. They had unearthed the paper-thin china teacups his father had bought out in China before the First World War and had dared to drink tea from them, served up with the crisply iced Fuller's cake Robert had brought over from Oban. To his surprise, the cups had not cracked. They had found all his father's notes from medical school in Glasgow and some cardboard pillboxes of medication. In a box in the attic, his mother had discovered shiny syringes and curled-up stethoscopes that smelled of perished rubber.

'I couldn't get rid of all this after he died,' she said. 'It wasn't quite time. But now...'

After tea they had sat leafing through a photo album with brown snaps of Robert's childhood. His parents had been privileged to have holidays abroad with their two children. Sometimes the family were pictured on cruises in places like Italy, Madeira or North Africa, posing by a palm tree or even holding a monkey. Sometimes they were on deck, wearing sun hats and playing quoits, or at the captain's table enjoying an elaborate meal. His mother clearly made a special effort for the evenings on these voyages; she was always the picture of elegance, with simple, fine jewellery and well-tailored dresses bought from her favourite Glasgow outfitters. Sometimes she was smoking a cigarette in a holder. He found this difficult to reconcile with the practical lady of later years who liked nothing better than to put on her boots and tweeds and climb up Heaval. She had devoted herself to helping her husband with the administration of the doctor's practice, but at weekends she had spent every moment in the fresh air.

The tide was coming in. Robert watched as the waves began to dislodge the stone circle in the sand. So much effort had been put into the way the stones had been spaced. In ten minutes they were covered.

He fingered the photographs in his pocket, the ones he hadn't spoken to his mother about. They had been at the back of the bureau drawer under a box of playing cards, in a small envelope labelled 'Melrose'. One was a sepia snapshot of a lady on horseback on a track by a wide river, labelled 'Mrs Gillespie, equestrienne'. In the background was an imposing country house with towers, which Robert recognised as Abbotsford in the Borders. When he had examined the photo with the magnifying glass, he had been startled to see the face of his mother. In another curled-up photo, she stood in front of a hotel doorway with a thin, dark-haired gentleman who wore plus fours and a tweed jacket. The gentleman was very handsome and had his arm round her. On the back of the photograph he had just been able to discern 'Mr and Mrs Andrew Gillespie', written in fading pencil.

'Mother,' Robert asked tentatively. 'Does the name Andrew Gillespie mean anything to you?'

They listened to the cry of the seagulls and watched the bobbing heads of two seals in the bay. His mother Mary clasped her hands, staring out to sea. She hastily touched the ring finger of her left hand.

The sun had slipped below the sea and the moon was rising. As they turned back to the cottage Mary began to talk.

The sun is setting as I walk up Craigpark. To the west are the great stone hulks of the Necropolis. Grand tombstones and obelisks pierce the skyline, but I can't look at those. I stop to draw breath, and turn towards the river Clyde glinting in the last pinkish rays of a weak April sun. It winds its way down past the shipyards to the Firth and then the open sea. I am proud to live in Glasgow, the second city of the Empire.

The lamplighter is outside the house. He doffs his cap as I arrive, and I nod in return. Our house is a sandstone end-terrace, purchased by my father five years ago with some of the proceeds from his successful wine and spirits business. The light glows in the dining room, and I see Mama framed in the window, fingering a lace tablecloth. And I stop, for I see that she is looking at the wedding gifts, her face reflected in a silver soup tureen of grand proportions. She is neat and tidy, her grey hair tied back in a bun, her reading spectacles at the end of her nose. She wears her best purple afternoon dress. I hesitate to disturb her; she is in harmony with her surroundings, and I will break that harmony.

I push open the door into the oak-panelled hallway that smells of stew and beeswax. My footsteps echo on the polished surround. I hang my coat and hat on the mahogany hallstand, peer into the mirror and pick up a comb. My face is thin, framed by long, dark hair. I hesitate to use the word gaunt, but that is the word that comes to mind. After I have tidied my appearance, I take the first door on the right, into the dining room.

'Oh Mary, there you are. I thought I'd make a start…' Mama looks at me. She has a faint air of embarrassment. I swallow.

'It is time, Mama. You know I feel better now.'

Mama is right. Now is the time. Over the winter I was ill; it was understandable, given the circumstances.

'I'll make a cup of tea, first.' She pats me gently on the shoulder. I stretch out my hands to the warmth of the fire which blazes in the blackened grate.

When she returns, we sit in silence and sip Darjeeling. Abby, our maid of work, has made some seed cake but I have little appetite for it.

Then Mama begins to tick the wedding presents off on her list.

'Six Edinburgh crystal sherry glasses… two silver sugar sifters… an embroidered tray cloth.'

I finger the tray cloth languidly, imagining myself a hostess. It has a delicate pattern of satin-stitch thistles which must have taken hours to work.

'Oh, that is beautifully done!' Mama cannot conceal her admiration. 'I believe Miss Paterson made it herself, so she did.'

I prise open the clasp of a rectangular wooden box. 'One case of fish knives and forks with ivory handles. From Mr and Mrs Provan.'

'Oh, and half a dozen knife rests. They're from Dr and Mrs Lawrie. Such a fine gift!' Mama looks up. 'Oh, now there's the postman with the evening delivery. Just see what he's brought, would you?'

I am grateful for the cool air of the hall. When I pick up the letters from the mat there is one written in an unfamiliar hand. The postmark is Paris. I struggle to think from whom it could be. And then I remember Edith. It is surely from Edith, and her mother Mrs Dorothy Markham! They were going to tour the Continent, were they not?

'Mary?'

I hesitate. I want time to read it on my own.

'Mary? I'm expecting a note from Violet Provan about the church social!' Mama's voice is insistent.

'Nothing for you, Mama,' I shout back. 'Just a note for me. Probably from Isa, about meeting in Miss Cranston's.' I slip the letter into my pocket.

When I return to the dining room Mama has been diverted by the presents again. She ticks another two items on her list and sighs.

&

I travel into town the following afternoon, the letter in my pocket. I have read it at least twenty times since yesterday. The tramcar creaks its way along Duke Street, past the Wellpark Brewery towards the city centre. I am going for my singing lesson with Miss Cameron in Kelvingrove. I turn over the tune of 'Eileen Alannah' in my head and practise my breathing. It has always been my ambition to sing for our little parties at home and, with regular nods from behind her Broadwood piano, Miss Cameron is encouraging me that I am improving. I put out a hand to the brass rail as the tram sways round a bend, and I imagine us all at home in the parlour. There I am at the piano in my green dress, ready to sing. The Provans and the McNicols are there, and the Campbells and James, of course, and my brother Bobby has brought Bella Fenwick, although Mama does not care for her. And there is an empty chair. I try not to think about that.

The tram squeals and creaks to a halt near Kelvingrove Park.

'C'moan an' get aff' noo!' The conductress yells the usual command and stands by the doors as I alight. I lift my skirt to ease my passage down the awkward steps and nod goodbye to her. She stands proud in her uniform and waves.

I am early for my lesson, so I stroll into the park and stop by the memorial fountain. The great red sandstone art gallery with its towers and pinnacles is to my right, and birds sing in the trees by the university. It is as if I have been asleep for a hundred years and have not noticed that the earth has come to life again. Some early, thin daffodils bloom in the borders and a young gardener greets me as he passes by.

I sit down on a park bench, and reach into my pocket for Edith's letter. Oh, how glad I am to hear from her! She writes that she and her mother are finishing their Continental tour in Glasgow in July and that we must meet before they sail back to New York.

My pulse quickens at the thought – they are such dear friends, but how can I tell them what happened?

Isa will know what to do. I will ask her when we meet after my singing lesson.

☙

Miss Cranston's in Sauchiehall Street is our favourite place in all of Glasgow. What a pleasure it is to have a quiet, elegant room in which to drink tea and converse with my lady friends! Isa and I meet every week in the Deluxe Room, designed by Mr Charles Rennie Mackintosh in the modern style. We have a favourite table by the window, where the light dapples gold patterns of the window's stained glass leaves on to the white table cloth. The room is light and bright, and yet the high-backed chairs give each table a sense of privacy. It is that privacy that I desire more than anything. I can share my secrets here.

'Guid efternoon, ladies, what can I get youse?'

The young waitress is small and pert, smartly dressed yet somehow not quite refined enough for Miss Cranston's.

'China tea for me, and one of the fruit scones. With straw-berry preserve,' I add.

The girl nods. Isa adjusts her hat. There is no denying she is pretty, with her blonde, freshly coiffed curls. It is a mystery that she has not been inundated with marriage proposals.

'China tea for me, too. And a scone.' Isa smiles at the waitress, then turns to me. 'How was your singing lesson, Mary? Oh, I forgot! I have a wee something for you.'

She reaches for her bag and fiddles with the clasp. She extracts her purse and opens it.

'It's a farthing. With this year's date… look, 1910! It will bring

41

you luck… better things…' Her hand shakes with a slight awkwardness. But her eyes cannot conceal her delight.

'Oh, Isa! What a beautiful thought! Thank you, indeed. Not everyone is like you. Why, only the other day Irene Douglas crossed the street when she saw me coming. Now, tell me, can you keep a secret?'

'You know I can!'

'It's this!' I take the letter from my pocket.

'Oh! A foreign stamp… let me see!'

'Yes! We're to have visitors. From America!'

'Oh, Mary! Whoever said our lives were dull!'

The waitress brings a silver teapot and some crockery in the willow pattern. I finger the edge of the plate and study the figures in the blue landscape of a distant land.

'But… Isa. I don't know. They met… Andrew… you see, when we were in Melrose.'

'I see.' She pauses and looks out of the window, then turns to me, trying to look brighter. 'So what have they been doing all this time? It's been nine months since…'

'A grand tour of Europe, evidently.'

We butter our scones and silently spread on the strawberry jam.

'I do want to see them. We had such a merry time together! But you and I need to think about what I say.'

My thoughts drift back to Melrose, as they often do. Outside the Deluxe Room, the sky is a glorious blue, the way it was that day before my life changed. We climbed the Eildon Hills at Melrose. Andrew was on the path behind me in his plus fours and tweed jacket. He'd stopped by the field gate to smoke his pipe, so I ran on over the heather towards the top. I could not believe how beautiful it was: the larks darting in the breeze, the bees on the heather, the patchwork of tiny fields at my feet. In the distance were the towers of Abbotsford, Sir Walter Scott's home. Andrew had said he would take me there on horseback the next day. I was thrilled of course, as I had never done such a thing. But first, he said, we had to see the whole of the Borderlands spread at our feet. We had to climb. I picked up the hem of my skirt and ran to the summit where I sat down in the heather and watched Andrew approach.

'Well, Mrs Gillespie? The outdoor life suits you. You're beautiful!'

'And you're out of breath!' We both laughed.

'Oh, I love it, Andrew! Look at the wee fields down there! I don't know how I'll feel about Glasgow after this. This is so different. I feel as if I could fly!'

'Well, Glasgow's our past and our future. My merchant's business. Things are going very well with the firm, you know. There has never been a better time for Glasgow! And our home… there's the flitting to organise when we get back.'

I thought of the new house being built for us in Dennistoun, not far from my parents' home in Craigpark. The rooms were light and airy; we had imitated the Mackintosh style in the designs for the windows and fireplaces. The paintwork was to be light instead of the usual dark stained wood.

'Oh yes, Andrew. The house… but, I can't explain it. Something about the wedding presents, maybe. A life of napery and silver knives!'

He smiled. 'A woman's place…'

'All generous gifts of course, but… I'd rather be out here!'

'We can go down the Clyde. Take the steamer to Dunoon in the summer.'

'And I'd probably still have to come home and make tea for Mama and Aunt Betty.' I visualised them admiring the embroidery on my napkins and exchanging recipes for gingerbread. 'No, I'd rather go further than Dunoon. Italy, maybe. And I'd like to work on my singing. Get better at it.'

'You will, Mary. And we'll explore together. We'll travel to the Continent. Come! You won't have to make scones today.' He reached for my hand.

I noticed he winced a little as he got up. I began to wonder then if there was something wrong. I was going to ask him when a young lady came running up. She was about my age, tall with chestnut brown hair loose about her shoulders and with a free, easy way of moving. Her shoes were unsuitable for climbing a hill, but that did not seem to trouble her.

'Oh my lord, that was real steep! My Mama said for sure she wouldn't do it! She's resting back at the hotel. Going round Melrose Abbey this morning sure tired her out, but I just wanted to rush right on up here and take it all in.' She stopped for breath and turned round, hands on hips, to admire the prospect. 'Say, is that Sir Walter Scott's house right over there? I so love his books! I get that real sense of Scotland from them.'

'Yes, the towers through the trees – that's Abbotsford.'

'I'm Edith, by the way. 'Edith Markham. My Mama and I are from America, from Boston. I'm not interrupting you two lovebirds, am I? Mama wondered if you were a honeymoon couple, when she saw you set off hand in hand from the hotel!'

Andrew smiled. 'We are, and proud of it. And I can truly recommend the married life. Meet my wife, Mrs Gillespie.'

'Mary,' I added.

'Andrew Gillespie.' Andrew offered his hand. 'Pleased to meet you, Edith.'

Mrs Markham, Edith's mother, was waiting outside the hotel when we got back down from the hill. It was all quite an ordeal, as our shoes had no grip on the rough path.

'There you are, Edith! I've been out here ages trying to see you up there on the hill. It kind of confused me, that there were three of you.' Her voice was deep and mellow. She spoke more slowly than her daughter. Their accents were fascinating.

Mrs Markham looked too young to be Edith's mother. When Edith had said her mother was resting, I had imagined someone much older, but they appeared more like sisters. She was beautifully dressed, in a comfortable kind of way, her grey dress of a light material.

Mrs Markham could not conceal her excitement. 'Oh, Edith! Such wonderful news! Mr McNab who owns the hotel here says he can arrange a ride in a motor-car tomorrow – to Dryburgh Abbey and Scott's View!' She turned to Andrew and myself.

'Say, would you folks like to join us?'

And so I had my first ride in a motor car, my face turned to the sun, the wind in my hair. Oh, Edith and Mrs Markham! How they hustled! But we felt their enthusiasm and saw the world with new eyes, somehow. They wanted to head right on to Kelso, but Andrew was looking tired, so they dropped us off at the hotel.

'Let's give these honeymooners a bit of time to themselves!'

Mrs Markham turned and waved as we closed the car door. I stood on the hotel steps, Andrew's hand in mine. Mr McNab, the hotel manager, said he would take a photograph of us if we would like it, and we agreed.

Isa lifts the pot and pours me another cup of tea. Her hand trembles slightly.

'You were miles away, Mary! Here, drink this!'

'I was remembering our drive in the motor car at Melrose and the sun on my face. Oh, and the time we went hill-walking, and horse-riding…' My voice sounds thin, distant.

'Oh, Mary…' She grips my hand tightly and smiles. 'Oh, how I'd love to take a drive like that! And to ride a horse! I'd love to travel. Do you know which countries Edith and Mrs Markham visited?'

'France, Italy, Switzerland. They went to Paris, I know. And Rome.'

'I can only dream of such places.' Isa leans back and sighs. She cuts her second scone with a pearl-handled knife. 'One of those great liners was departing from the docks today when I travelled into town. I could only stop and stare! It wasn't just the size of it, it was all these people sailing off, seeking a new life.'

'My brother Bobby wants to do that, you know. He does not dare tell Mama and Papa, as he is sure they will not be pleased. And I am not so sure how I feel about it either. I believe in keeping the family close.'

'Of course.' Isa nods.

⁕⁊

Mama is darning by the fire when I return from town. She has a substantial pile of grey socks which belong to my father and my brother Bobby.

'Ah, Mary, there you are!' Her face brightens. 'Was Miss Cameron pleased with your singing?'

'Oh yes! She spoke well of my singing, Mama. And I have a new song, 'Where Corals Lie', by Mr Edward Elgar.'

Mama purses her lips. 'Well, that will be about some far-flung place, no doubt. I've had quite an afternoon of it. The woman that came round about the maid's job was no use. Stout wasn't the word for it, and untidy too. "Well, if I dinnae suit, ma'am, I cannae work for youse." That's what she said when I remarked on her appearance.'

We both enjoy a moment of shared laughter. Mama relaxes slightly.

'You must have been glad she decided it herself,' I observe.

'I was indeed, have no fear! But then here I am with a pile of darning I will never finish! And all the silver to clean. Such a pity that Abby has to get married.'

Abby, our maid of work for the past five years, is to depart next week to marry a Mr John Macgregor from the South Side. There is no question of her carrying on her work with us.

'Oh, we will miss her,' I reflect. 'But I hope she will be happy…'

Mama hesitates. 'I checked through some more of the wedding presents. Look at this exquisite firescreen! To think Mrs Marr did all that cross-stitch! Oh, and these mother-of-pearl tea knives look so well on the mahogany table…'

I do not want to look at the presents today. My mouth is dry and my heart is beating faster, but I know I must tell Mama about Edith.

'Mama, I received a letter.'

'Well, you often receive letters, Mary.'

'This one was posted in Paris.'

'Fancy! Now who would that be? Could you just pass me those afternoon serviettes. I want to see how Ada did that embroidery round the edge.'

'It's from Edith, Mama. And her mother, Mrs Dorothy Markham. You remember? The Americans we met in the hotel at Melrose.'

'Oh yes! They must have met… you both.' Mama puts down the napkins.

'They are coming to Glasgow. In the summer. July.'

'Well, they must come for tea. I'll get out the Crown Derby for them.'

'Oh, I'm sure they will love to come to us. But I think I will take them to Miss Cranston's first. Because, you see, they do not know what happened after they left Melrose… I cannot imagine how I will tell them.'

'Well, you know best, my dear. Under the circumstances. But we must welcome them here at Dennistoun. I have a new recipe for gingerbread. Perhaps James Campbell would like to join us? And the Provans? I could set up a little party, and you could sing that corals song for us.'

'I think James is very busy with his work just now. He has his final papers coming up at the University.'

'Och, he does enjoy your company, though.' Mama puts down her darning, casting a glance at the clock on the mantelpiece. 'Goodness, it's half past six! I must get on with the supper. Where has the time gone?'

Papa is a man of habit. He works for six days a week. On Sundays he rests and accompanies us to two church services. He returns on weekday evenings at six and goes straight to the kitchen, where he discusses the day's events with Mama before supper. Tonight he is half an hour later than usual, and I hear him talk with Mama for a long time. And I know that they will be discussing Andrew's father, the Reverend Gillespie. Papa was to go and see him after work.

I know that they are discussing money. And I do not really like that I am not involved, because it does concern me, after all.

It has always been thus. Things not meant for our ears are discussed in the kitchen, with the door closed. Or in their bedroom on the first floor. Last night I am sure they discussed Bobby, and how they would like him to work in the family business. Today I know it is my future that is debated.

☙

Sometimes in the late afternoon I walk in Alexandra Park. It is not the same as walking in the countryside, but I know that the exercise does me good. When I stroll among the trees and flowering plants, I almost feel well again, but a weariness often descends on me as I approach our home. One day the kitchen door is closed when I arrive. I hear the raised voices of Mama, Papa, and Bobby, and I go to my room, knowing that they wish to be private. Half an hour later, the front door slams and I see

Bobby leave in quite a hurry. I imagine that he is heading for Bella's home for tea. I descend to the hall just in time to hear Papa shout that he is going out to walk in the park, and I am startled by this departure from his routine.

I follow Mama into the parlour, where she picks up her knitting. Her hands tremble and her needles click more loudly than usual.

'Sometimes I think you will all desert me! There's your brother Willie just moved out to Netherton, and now, believe it or not, here is Bobby saying he is going to marry Bella Fenwick and that they may go to the far reaches of the Empire! To Canada, if you please! Poke the fire, would you, Mary? Those coals are not catching. Now, Abby always set a good fire.'

'Marry Bella? You cannot say that you did not see this coming, Mama! If she is his choice...'

'But she is not strong. Perhaps she will not bear children... and, even if she does, I would never see them if they are to go to Canada!'

I poke the fire vigorously, relishing the percussion of metal on coal.

'We all thought Bobby would follow your father into the business!' Mama is quiet for a moment. 'Oh, Mary, I'm so glad to have you here. These evenings by the fire are so comfortable.'

'Mama, it unsettles me too, thinking of our going separate ways. But then I think of Andrew, and I think we must take our opportunities.'

'We must trust in the Lord. That's what we must do! Why, I was reading in the *Quiver* only the other day how He shows us the way. There it is over there, Mary.' She indicates the corner table. 'You would do well to read the article. He will open the door that you seek. He will, indeed.'

The coals begin to catch light and spark.

I feel suddenly bolder. 'Mama, He closed a door for me. I want to try opening my own doors.'

'Goodness, you do have some strange ideas! What would your Papa say?'

'And... I am troubled about the Reverend Gillespie. Why does he not talk to me directly about the money?'

'Well, it's a matter for the men, and that's that. We need not concern our heads with it, thank the Lord.'

'But it's my future!'

'The Lord will see us right, Mary. Can you just pass me that hank of wool? Yes, the fawn one. Thank you. Have you prepared your lesson for the Mission on Sunday? James Campbell said he would call round after evening church, you know.'

In my room I finger the pages of the Mission booklet, dreading the approaching Sunday. I stand at the window, where I can just see the river. And if I open the window I can hear the horns of the ships on the Clyde.

ᴇↃ

The Free Church of Scotland in Craigpark is an imposing building. We make our way there every Sunday morning, and again on Sunday evening. It is our routine. We dress in our finery and walk down the hill, nodding at friends and acquaintances on the way – the Provans, the Campbells, the McVeys, and other residents of Craigpark.

The Reverend Carroll always preaches a good sermon. Sometimes I discuss them with James Campbell on the way home. But I suppose that most of all I regard the hour at church as a time of reflection. From our seat in the gallery, I survey the congregation. I smell the pitch pine of the polished pews, and the peppermints sucked during long sermons. Sometimes I think of my own situation and I look down at my hands clasped in my lap. But sometimes I look up at the pointed arches of the windows. And when the organ stirs and we sing the hymn 'We have an anchor', I hear Mama's advice in my head, saying that the Lord will help us. I watch James Campbell and his family in their pew, and I think of his medical studies, and I wonder if he can help me with my question.

The organ plays the processional, and we walk out into the May sunshine, a clutch of figures in the dark shades of Sunday best.

'May I walk you home, Mary?' It is the soft, Highland voice of James. He doffs his hat.

'You may, James.'

Mama nods in the background, as if encouraging us. James and I turn up the hill and soon we have left our parents, who linger to talk to the Provans at the church door.

'Will I see you later this evening? Are you helping at the Mission?' I ask.

'Yes, I will be there at six.'

'Oh, James, it is hard to say this. But I dread it. I don't have it in me to teach a Bible class, but Mama and Papa insist on it. Those boys are so badly behaved. But I must prepare my lesson better, I know it. Oh, if I could make up my own mind I think

I would not do it.'

'But you can be making up your own mind.'

We stop in front of the Post Office. I look up at him. He is tall and there is a look of sympathy and understanding in those dark eyes. I straighten my back, raising myself up to return his gaze.

'I am beginning to think I can. James, there is something I have wanted to ask you. For a long time.'

'And what might that be?'

'With your medical knowledge, you see. Could I have saved Andrew? If I had known sooner? Mr McNab, the hotel proprietor, alerted the doctor straight away in the night, when Andrew had the pain. It was so severe. He was crippled with it, sweating…'

Suddenly the words won't come any more. I hesitate, on the brink of tears. I do not want James to see my emotion so clearly.

His hand is on my shoulder. 'Mary, if it pains you, you must not speak of it. You are only recently recovered from your own illness…'

'No, I must know. In the days before he took ill, Andrew was sometimes pale, sometimes tired. I should have said something.'

'Mary, you did all you could. A perforated appendix can happen very suddenly. It is very serious, and even if we can consider surgery, the patients do not always survive the rigours of the operation.'

'I understand. James, sometimes I see Andrew's face. Sometimes I imagine he is telling me what I should do.' I hesitate, then decide to mention my other concern. 'And there is a problem with Andrew's father.'

'His father is a man of the Kirk, is he not?'

'He is indeed. But he is a poor man of the Kirk. And he has been to Papa and, you see… I am not sure if I should say this… from the will I have inherited all Andrew's money, and his father does not like it.'

'Oh, Mary…'

'But the real problem is that Mr Gillespie does not talk to me! He talks to Papa. And I also keep wondering if Mr Gillespie avoids me because he thinks I could have saved Andrew.'

'Be assured on both counts, Mary. I have told you; you could have done no more for Andrew than you did. And as for the money, I think in law it is yours if the will says it. You need not be worrying yourself. Andrew loved you dearly. He left the money to you, his wife.'

I swallow. 'That is good, thank you.'

'But I see from your face that it still concerns you.'

We reach our front door. I give him my hand.

'Thank you, James. This has helped me more than you must realise. Mama and Papa are very supportive and have taken me back home, but slipping into my old routine is not straight-forward, as you can imagine.'

'I know, Mary. But you can find your own way.' He nods and lifts his hat. Then he is gone round the corner in the direction of Alexandra Road.

❧

The trees wear their heavy, July foliage as I set off to catch the tramcar into town. It is a warm day, and a blue sky studded with pearly clouds will welcome my visitors. They will see Glasgow at its best.

In the great concourse of Queen Street station, I pick some smuts off my fawn jacket and adjust the position of my hat. I do not wear black now. It made me feel so miserable, so ill. There is almost a spring in my step as I walk through the station; it is a long time since I have felt such vigour. The trains coming and going fill me with excitement; the platforms vibrate with the noise of them, and the air is filled with clouds of steam. I walk towards the platform where the Edinburgh train has just come in. Carriage doors swing open, and I strain to see the familiar figures of the tall young woman and her mother.

Then Edith is there, waving. She runs, as she always did. She looks tanned and well and is wearing a smart, light green coat and hat.

'Mary! How wonderful to see you! You look well, but... thinner.'

Mrs Markham emerges smiling from the carriage, stepping carefully down on to the platform. She is slightly stooped. I rush to help her.

'Oh, Mary! We are so excited to be reunited with you. But... are you on your own?' She takes both my hands and holds them in hers for a long time.

'I can't wait to hear about the places you've seen—'

'Oh, but I want to see this beautiful Glasgow straight away,' Edith interrupts me in her excitement. 'Can we get a cab to our hotel? It's the Windsor. Is there a porter around here?'

I alert a porter, who helps Edith and Mrs Markham transport

a succession of hatboxes and trunks to the waiting cab. The black horses paw the ground, eager to be off. The driver whistles as he helps us in. We settle into our seats.

'Where is Andrew, Mary? Is he well?' Edith puts her hand on my arm. I use the excitement of the first turn into George Square to divert attention from Edith's question, and point out further landmarks on the way to the Windsor Hotel in St Vincent Street. Edith reaches into her bag and reads from her Bradshaw's Guide. Bradshaw, it seems, considers Glasgow one of the most splendid cities of Europe.

'It is "not surpassed for beauty of architecture even by Edinburgh itself". That's what he says. I find that real hard to believe! We visited all the sights of Edinburgh and they were sensational. Holyrood, the Castle, the Royal Mile…'

'Ah, but you will see what Glasgow has to offer. We will go to Kelvingrove and Glasgow Green, of course, but after you have settled into your rooms I would like to take you somewhere very special – Miss Cranston's Ladies' Tearoom.' I know they will be thrilled with Miss Cranston's.

'A Ladies' Tearoom! Oh yes, please, Mary!' Edith coos as we draw up at the Windsor.

'Aye, Glasgow's a bonnier city than Edinburgh,' the cab driver remarks tersely, as he begins the task of unloading the trunks. I nod to him to wait until we are ready to go on to Sauchiehall Street.

એ

Edith cannot get over the splendour of the Deluxe Room.

'So this is the tearoom that Mr Charles Rennie Mackintosh designed! This purple and white – it's just beautiful! All that intricate glasswork on the doors and windows…'

Mrs Markham surveys the room. 'Would you take a look at the high backs of those chairs! The proportions seem kind of wrong to me but, when I sit here at the table, I feel all enclosed. As if we can whisper secrets!'

I take my cue.

'I have something to tell you, ladies.'

'Guid efternoon, ladies. What can I get youse?' The waitress hovers by the table with her pencil and pad.

'I do recommend the scones. And the teacake is also delicious,' I say hurriedly, hoping they do not notice that I am somewhat flustered.

'Well, let's have scones AND teacake!' Edith says.

I choose my moment after the waitress has departed.

'Edith, Mrs Markham, I have something to tell you…'

'Oh my, how do you pronounce this street name?' Edith has got out the Bradshaw again. 'Where this tearoom is?'

'It's Sauchiehall. Sauchiehall Street.'

'Socky Hall!' Edith laughs and tries to imitate my pronunciation. 'Wonderful!'

'It means street of the willows. There used to be willow trees here once. Weeping willows.' I stare out of the window, imagining a green pasture with curtains of willows shimmering in the breeze. Outside the pavements are hard and cold.

Edith interrupts my reverie. 'You have something to tell us, Mary.'

'It's about Andrew.'

'He'll join us later, maybe? I mean he can't come here, it's a ladies' tearoom!'

And then I tell them. I tell them that Andrew died.

'So there's a wee selection of scones and cakes for youse.' The waitress places a silver cake stand in the centre of the table, and stands proudly to attention, awaiting our praise.

I hear the chink of crockery, the high-pitched buzz of ladies' conversation, the exchange of everyday gossip. Edith's and Mrs Markham's faces seem frozen. For once, their chatter is silenced. Then Edith takes my hand.

'Oh, Mary!'

Mrs Markham's arm is round my shoulder. 'Oh, my dear!'

There are tears in my eyes, but I swallow hard and regain my composure.

'It's been nearly ten months now. And sometimes it becomes easier. I had to… pick up my old life.'

'Mary, I don't know what to say.' Edith reaches into her bag for a handkerchief. 'I've come over kind of faint.'

Mrs Markham keeps her arm round my shoulders. It is comforting, warm. 'Mary, I lost my Adrian, you know. You cannot believe you will never see them again. That is the cruelty of it. But you will live a little more in due course, you will see.' She takes a sip of tea. 'But what happened?'

'It was appendicitis – a perforated appendix. Very sudden. He died at Melrose. A few days after you left. A few days after our ride in the motor car.'

I sip my tea and think back to that day when we laughed in the sun and when Andrew and I thought we had all our lives before us. And I know that Edith and Dorothy will help me.

❧

Some days later I struggle against the wind as I walk up Lawrence Street. It has begun to rain and, even though it is summer, the wind has blown leaves and twigs onto the pavement. I also struggle with my inner feelings and my decision. I pass East Partick Church and glance at my watch; I have two hours before my singing lesson with Miss Cameron. Surely this is enough to say what I have to say?

Andrew's father, the Reverend Gillespie, minister of East Partick, lives with his housekeeper in a ground floor flat at 23 Lawrence Street. Andrew's mother died when he was ten and he talked little of her. We visited the house regularly when we were courting, but I have hardly seen Mr Gillespie since Andrew's death.

I stand at the dark brown doorway with its cracked paint, gripping my music case tightly, and I ring the bell.

'Mary!'

Mr Gillespie himself answers the door. His housekeeper Miss McPherson is evidently occupied in the kitchen; I hear banging and clattering from the far end of the hall. He frowns and hesitates, puzzled to see me alone.

'Mr Gillespie! I hope you don't mind my calling unannounced. I am on my way to my singing lesson. I won't take up much of your time.'

He opens the door an inch wider. It creaks on hinges that beg for oil.

'Come in, Mary! Do come in!' He slowly swings the door open and shakes my hand awkwardly.

I follow the stooped figure into the bare hallway with its lingering smell of fish custard, Miss McPherson's favourite dish. Our footsteps echo on the red and black mosaic tiles. I hear the sound of water running and dishes being washed in the kitchen. Mr Gillespie motions me into the parlour, a well-proportioned room with a bay window, sparsely furnished.

'Mary! I was talking to your father only the other day. But to see you… are you quite on your own? Are you well? Will you have some tea?'

Overwhelmed by the sudden rush of questions, I sit down on the black horsehair couch.

'Yes, thank you. I am as well as can be expected, Mr Gillespie. And you?

'Aye, I am well, Mary.' When he turns to me I can see his face is more lined than I remembered. He has a distant, distracted look. The elbows of his black jacket are worn shiny from hours of work at his desk in the corner. He lifts a small brass bell and rings for Miss McPherson. Dressed all in black with a white apron, her grey hair neatly tied back, she hovers in the doorway, eyes wide.

'Mary! How are you, my dear? And your parents? It has been a wee while…'

Her warmth eases the tense atmosphere in the parlour, and Mr Gillespie settles himself into his chair by the fireplace. The empty marble grate is concealed by a tapestry firescreen. The brass of the companion set is dull. We talk of the weather and the current vogue for emigration to Canada. I do not mention my brother Bobby.

'I felt it was time I spoke with you. We have both… lost

a dear one.' I turn the conversation to more important matters.

'And I have lost three dear ones, Mary.' He clears his throat. 'My only brother, Hector, who ran the merchant's business with Andrew… the business which Andrew inherited after my brother died.' He sighs. 'And of course my wife Betty, who passed away all those years ago…' He nods at a small photograph on his desk.

'I am sorry, indeed.'

'Aye, the ways of the Lord are hard to comprehend at times.'

He stares at the fireside rug. Miss McPherson arrives with a tray of tea and cake. She lays it quietly on a side table and slips out, closing the door behind her.

'You have talked much with my father.'

'I have, Mary. You see, I live humbly.' He glances around the room. 'I cannot afford much. Andrew did well with my brother's business. And your family, if I may say…' He breaks off, evidently finding it too awkward to carry on. 'Would you care for some cake?'

I take a piece of Madeira cake and cut it into small pieces with a silver-handled knife. It is dry and crumbly, and I fear I shall choke on it. Mr Gillespie pours us each a cup of tea before he continues.

'Mary, I have a proposal which I have outlined to your father. I think he will find it reasonable in the circumstances of the estate.'

'*He* will find it reasonable! And will I?'

Mr Gillespie rises from his chair and begins to pace the room, finally stopping by the window, where he turns his back on me.

A mahogany clock ticks loudly on the mantelpiece; I fancy I can see the hands move, so long is the silence between us.

At length he turns to me. I stand up.

'May I make a proposal?' I say, as firmly as I dare.

'A proposal! Young ladies do not often make proposals! I must say I am surprised that you address me in this way, Mary. Sit down. Pray, sit down. Your father and I have done our best to protect you from the difficulties of the situation. You were, understandably, somewhat unwell for a time.'

I take two steps towards him.

'And I am grateful for that kindness. I am now recovered, and my concern is not with your reasonable request, which my father has now informed me of. My concern is that you think I have not a tongue in my head, nor a wish in my heart.'

'Mary! That is enough!' He sits down, his shoulders trembling.

To my surprise, there are tears in his eyes when he looks up at me.

'Oh, Andrew! Why, Mary? Why did he die?'

Softly I rest my hand on his shoulder. 'Mr Gillespie, we have both lost Andrew. Do you not realise that I have been asking myself what Andrew would have wanted. For us both?'

'Oh, Mary…'

'And be assured that all was done at Melrose to save Andrew's life. I am confident of that. He had the best physician, and the McNabs at the hotel could not have been kinder. Now listen to my proposal.'

We talk for a further half hour and, when I go to my singing lesson, Miss Cameron says that I sing 'Where Corals Lie' more beautifully than I have ever done before.

❧

It has been awkward since I have told Mama and Papa of the decisions I have made.

Mama sits at the dining room table. She marks off the last of the wedding presents to be returned.

'Two brass candlesticks from Mrs McNaughton. They would have needed a lot of cleaning, anyway,' she tuts.

'So the list is complete, Mama. It was not easy. But we had to do it.'

Silence falls between us. Mama goes to her chair by the fire and picks up the *Quiver*. She leafs through the pages of the magazine, then puts it down. When she looks up, I see dark circles beneath her eyes. She has not slept well for some time.

'This venture of yours, this voyage to America! Mary, I don't know how I shall cope!'

I clear my throat. 'I shall miss home, miss the family of course.'

'How can you leave us! Such an outlandish idea!'

'It is not for ever, Mama.' My heart is beating faster. My palms sweat.

'A year is an eternity. It is indeed! Please, Mary?'

I walk to the window and glance down the hill, scanning Craigpark Road for the postman.

I can stay in this routine, or I can go.

'Mama, I have thought long about this. I am sometimes fearful of the future, but I will pray to the Lord.'

Mama nods in approval. 'Oh, indeed you must. And I will pray for you every day.' She picks up her knitting, a waistcoat for my father, and fiddles with the end of the ball of wool. 'One thing does comfort me. I do like Edith and Mrs Markham. And what you did for the Reverend Gillespie... yes, that was good. Although I hear he was shocked that you went out to Partick to talk to him yourself. Your Papa could have seen to it, you know.'

'I am glad that I did, Mama. And just think, there is one other thing that comforts you.'

'Oh yes! I am pleased indeed that Bobby has thought better of his plans to emigrate. He will take a role in the family business, as he should. Much better than the wildwoods of Nova Scotia, to be sure.'

'And... you will have a new daughter-in-law to keep you company!'

'Oh, Bella Fenwick! Mary, can you not stay?'

I watch the postman approach and listen for the clatter of the letterbox, eager for an opportunity to leave the stifling heat of the room.

෴

I sit on my favourite bench by the fountain in Kelvingrove Park, wondering if James will come. I have seen little of him recently; he has been away on holiday with his parents since passing his final examinations at the University Medical School. I have not forgotten his kindness and his advice about Andrew, and I wish to thank him.

The clock strikes two, then the quarter hour. I watch a young couple idly push their baby carriage through the park. Some girls skip and play singing games on the grass. And then James appears, running towards me, his hat in his hand.

'Oh, James! I am so glad you have come. I thought for a moment you must not have got my postcard.' I am on my feet. He takes my hand.

'I did receive it, Mary, and I apologise for my lateness. My professor at the university wished to talk to me about something important.'

'And now you are Doctor Campbell! I am so proud of you. And of the good work you will do in the world. Come, let us walk through the park. And then perhaps we can have tea in town to celebrate your success?'

'Certainly. But Mary, tell me about yourself. It has been some time since we met. This is not the only reason for your summons, is it? To congratulate me on my success? You must have something else to relate, I am sure! Before you depart for America…'

'I wanted to thank you, James. For your help and advice.' I hesitate. 'And America, James… I think I am not going, after all. I decided it last night. My place is here in Glasgow, with the family. I cannot do this to them! Mama would suffer terribly! And we have still not engaged a new maid. None is to Mama's taste. Papa would miss me too, of course.'

We pass some children playing hopscotch, and I wish I was young again and that my life was uncomplicated.

'But you were decided, Mary! And you have Edith and Mrs Markham as companions! Have you told them of your decision?'

'I have not, as yet, but my mind is made up. They are dear friends. They will understand.'

'I do not think they will.' The corners of James's mouth twitch. 'We talked of opportunities, of doors opening. Come, let us sit down.' He guides me towards a bench in the shade of a beech tree.

'I have such an opportunity myself, Mary.'

'You do?'

'My professor says there are positions for ship's doctors. For a year.'

'You would travel? Oh, James! To America, perhaps?

'To the Orient.'

'Oh! So far away! Would there not be dangers? And the risk of disease…'

He laughs. 'Disease is my profession. I can hardly run away from it! Oh, it is an opportunity for me. And one which I think I shall take. It will further my experience, and I shall be of value in the world, as you point out.'

Despite his worthy intentions, I feel a strange wave of dizziness come over me. The park moves around me, and I grip the side of the bench.

'Consider it carefully, James.'

'I shall do it. Some distance will help me consider my future here in Glasgow. Oh, and I shall return. It is not for ever. Now come, let us have tea.'

He takes my arm and we walk through the park gates towards Sauchiehall Street.

༄

Seagulls wheel in the weak morning sunlight. I close my eyes, sniffing engine oil and the salt of the sea. I listen to the metallic clatter of horses' hooves, the unloading of trunks and the buzz of excited conversation. The dark grey, oily sea laps and sucks at the sides of the ship, and I wonder if I will be a good sailor.

Mrs Markham is sitting on her trunk, dressed in a new coat from Copland and Lye which I helped her choose. I, too, have a new travelling outfit, in deep blue. The SS *Columbia* of the Anchor Line towers over us. I have never felt so nervous in my life. We stand among jostling crowds in the shadow of the great ship, waiting for Captain Walter Baxter to welcome us on board. My ticket for the Anchor Line has cost me eight pounds, but of course I can afford it. I finger it nervously. I feel the touch of Edith's arm round my waist and turn to see her smiling face.

'They say he's real handsome, Captain Baxter.' Edith smiles. 'Mary, we are so happy you are coming. It makes our departure from your beautiful country less sad. But of course, I am eager to be at home and see my friends. And you will meet them all in due course.'

Mama, Papa and my brothers stand to my right, dressed in their Sunday best. Bobby stands protectively beside Bella, who fiddles nervously with her bonnet ribbons. Willie has come in specially from the farm at Netherton with his wife Maisie. We converse little; there does not seem to be much to say. As a parting gift, they have given me a beautifully illustrated Bible, which they have all signed.

'Mary! Mary!'

I hear running footsteps behind me, and suddenly there is Isa, radiant, dishevelled and out of breath.

The foghorn blasts, making us all jump. Mama puts her hand on her chest.

'Isa! You came!' We embrace, and I feel something of her strength and enthusiasm transfer to me.

'America! How I wish I could come with you. But... I know you want to do this on your own.'

'Oh, Isa, I am glad you said it. Yes, I do want to go. I dithered so long. Mama, the family... and James... but now I am sure. I will go. And it will help me consider my future here in Glasgow.'

'Do you have the lucky farthing?'

'I do.'

I fetch the farthing from my pocket und hold it up.

Mr Gillespie has been standing in the background, near Papa. He comes forward to give me his hand.

'Mary, I cannot let you go without thanking you. It is a generous amount, indeed.'

I am relieved. 'As you know, Andrew left me comfortably off. I am glad to have organised it.'

'It is indeed for the best, that your family takes over Andrew's business. Your father has a shrewd business sense.'

'But I will take an interest too.' I glance over at Papa, who has turned the other way.

'I wish you well, Mary. Andrew always wanted to travel—'

Mr Gillespie is cut off by another abrupt blast of the foghorn. There is a wave of movement in the crowd, as the passengers begin to embark. He pats me on the shoulder, then disappears into the crowd.

I embrace each family member. Papa helps Mama to a nearby bench. Then I turn and climb the creaking gangway that leads upwards to the passenger deck. It seems as if it will never end and I will be forever suspended between land and sea. When we finally stand on the polished boards of the deck, I grip the handrail and wave to the small group of friends and family far below.

James is not there. I watched his boat leave for China last week.

The anchor is lifted, the ship vibrates beneath my feet and, when the waving figures on the quayside become tiny dots, I turn my face to the wind.

Mary Campbell had put a haunting song by Elgar on the gramophone in the corner. Robert sat quietly with his mother, listening to the rise and fall of the alto voice singing 'Where Corals Lie'. The living room of the cottage was stripped almost bare. They sat in two chairs by the window, looking at the pier where the boat would depart next day for Oban. There was hardly a ripple on the water, and they watched the progress of a small rowing boat heading for Kisimul Castle in the early evening light.

The grandfather clock in the hall struck six, its chimes echoing through the empty cottage. Mary got up and filled two glasses with Harvey's Bristol Cream; they were the Edinburgh crystal ones that she had always liked best. She had wanted to pack them last.

'They were original wedding presents. From my marriage with Andrew. I can tell you that now.' Mary lightly touched his arm.

'I thought you returned all the gifts.'

'Not quite all. Some people asked us to keep them. It was all so awkward, really. Some went to your Uncle Bobby and Aunt Bella. I got another set of presents, of course, when I married your father.' Mary began to sip her sherry.

Robert held the glass up to the light and sniffed the sticky, amber liquid. He had always preferred dry sherry. They clinked glasses.

'To our future, Mother.' He paused. 'I knew you'd gone to America, of course, but I never knew what prompted it. This whole story…' He took a sip of sherry, winced and placed the glass on the table. 'It's so hard to take in. Poor Andrew. And how you must have suffered. I can't begin to imagine it!'

'America gave me distance, Robert. And time. And then I moved into my new life when I was ready. I returned to Glasgow from Boston before the war broke out, but of course your father was away as an army doctor in France all those years. You know all that. We wrote to each other, your father and I. For me it was the greatest miracle of all that he survived the war. I knew, finally, in 1918 that I would be the doctor's wife. My luck had turned. I was surrounded by so many widows, and I felt for them of course…'

'And I am the doctor's son.' Robert pondered the tenuous chain of events that had led to his birth. He had begun to see his mother in a new light, a strong woman who had striven for independence in an age that did not permit it. The marriage with his father had given her more than a life of domesticity; it had been her great joy to help with the patients, the paperwork and the prescriptions. 'I feel fulfilled here' is what she always used to say. Now he understood her.

'Your Uncle Bobby and Aunt Bella moved into the house that Andrew and I had built,' Mary said.

'Aunt Bella's house? To think of the number of times I've been there!'

Robert had never known his Uncle Bobby, who had been killed towards the end of the Great War, but he was still a regular visitor at his Aunt Bella's home in Dennistoun and was on good terms with his three cousins.

'And Edith?'

'She will be sailing up the Clyde with her daughter in exactly six weeks. From New York.' Mary put down her empty glass. 'Now come. Let us have one final walk to the beach.'

They sat long by the shore, their eyes on the western horizon, listening to the whisper of the waves.

Pinion of wild

❧

Horse-riding in the Sierra Nevada

It eats please slowly, its table is not rented,' Ian says ponderously.

He points to the phrase at the head of a list of dishes that a TV cookery show would describe as 'rustic'. The hand of Google translate is evident. We take it to mean 'enjoy your meal and take your time' and settle down for the evening.

A few young men with low-slung jeans are drinking and laughing at the bar, but we're the only customers in for dinner. Hearing us speak English, the waitress has handed over the English menu with great reverence. It's their only one, she says, smiling. There's a welcoming fire in the corner, but our voices echo in the dining room with its vaulted ceiling and floor of ceramic tiles. They're that terracotta colour with navy blue that you tend to associate with Spain.

It's been a long day: a flight to Granada, then a taxi through a red, arid landscape on the way east to the town of Guadix. Towering cliffs and pillars of weathered tufa make it look like the Wild West. Then we notice the white chimneys poking like periscopes out of the ground; they make us feel we're being watched. They belong to cave houses with whitewashed walls to the street; behind their firmly shut doors they tunnel deep into the hillside, concealing their inhabitants. The suburb of Barrio Santiago is piled up chaotically on the slopes above the town, surrounded by eerie, conical rocks sculpted by winds from the Sierra Nevada. The mountains in the distance are still capped with snow, even though it's late April.

We're at the Tio Tobas cave apartments in Alcudia de Guadix, far away from the *costas* and English food. Our cave is furnished simply in local style, and I'm pleased to say we have one window. It faces the Sierra Nevada and the bins, where a thin dog sleeps in the early spring sun. *Ormigas* is the first new Spanish word we've learned here; we've just finished spraying the ants on the windowsill and are hoping they will have expired by the time we're back from the restaurant.

Ian is frowning over the menu, which features something called luff, salad of canons, roast pinion of wild, beef to the cream and ox to the stone.

'Lamb to the slaughter,' I say. 'That's us tomorrow.'

We ask for the Spanish menu, which is readily comprehensible. 'To the' seems to be 'à la', as in Chicken à la King.

'Buey a la piedra. Ox to the stone,' I say. 'Let's have that.'

'To Juan,' says Ian, holding up his glass of Rioja. 'The best riding teacher in Spain.'

I'm not in my element. I'm sitting next morning at the window of what I'd really call a transport café, with a Lipton's tea bag in a glass of hot water. The water isn't quite hot enough, so the amber colour of the tea doesn't spread right up to the top of the glass. Cigarette smoke hangs in the air, mixed with the savoury aromas of last night's cooking. Across the road from

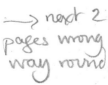
—> next 2 pages wrong way round

it's one of those where the eyes follow you around the room, and he's just seen Marta win some coins. Their clatter drowns out the television which no-one is watching. There's something on about a volcano in Iceland with a long name. Marta hasn't thought of sweeping up last night's olive stones from the floor by the bar; there's too much to enjoy, in a lazy, contented way.

Juan hasn't officially started his day's work, so all we've had is a smile and a brief '*Hola*'. A whiff of leather, horses and aftershave precedes him, and he has an aura of health and energy that is difficult to reconcile with his breakfast of black coffee and a cigarette. He gestures to the door. We pick up our riding helmets and follow.

They don't wear riding helmets in Spain. Juan is ahead of us on the trail. In his checked shirt, jeans and cowboy hat, he looks like the old adverts for Marlboro cigarettes. He sits astride his horse, twisting round from time to time to check on us. Now he's on his mobile phone, arranging a Saturday night date with a lady in Guadix. He tells us of the hidden benefits of horse riding for one's sex life.

'For a man, it also massage the *próstata*. Is good,' he adds.

'Too much information,' says Ian, proud to pronounce it the Spanish way. In-for-ma-thee-on.

I have nothing to add.

We are looking very English, red-faced and sweating under the riding hats, thinking about good posture and discouraging the horses from eating olive leaves, which apparently cause flatulence. Juan has indicated this effectively by mime. We've already been complimented on our 'bal*ance*' and have followed his terse

Café Peña are Juan's riding stables or, more accurately, his riding caves; a few wiry horses frisk in the arena, sending up clouds of ochre dust. The view is gradually obscured by each new truck that parks in the rough forecourt, the screech of tyres and the slamming of doors startling the dog that has followed us down from the cave. Breakfast time is rush hour.

We're wearing jodhpurs and chaps. I'm not quite sure how this happened; one minute Ian was saying that everyone needed to learn to ride before the day when the petrol runs out, and the next minute our flights were booked. As I chew on the dry ham sandwich which is my breakfast, I feel my shoulders tighten; this isn't going to be like trotting round the riding school at Larkrigg Farm, working up to the occasional canter in the last five minutes of the hour. The word 'gallop' was mentioned over last night's ox to the stone and I've had an uneasy first night in the cave. We have also decided that the 'all year round ambient temperature of 18 degrees', which is apparently a feature of these dwellings, is probably best appreciated in summer.

Juan sits on a bar stool, reading *El País*. He's chatting intermittently with Marta, the café owner, a cigarette in his hand. He's about fifty, or maybe younger, with a moustache, his brown hair streaked with grey. Marta looks about the same age; they have an easy familiarity which has apparently been built up over many such breakfasts. Her black hair is pulled back into a neat bun, and she wears glasses to operate the coffee machine. She is also enjoying a cigarette, taking the time to chat with Juan about the morning's news and casually playing with a bleeping one-armed bandit when the conversation dries up. Behind the bar there's a picture of Jesus with a crown of thorns;

commands to 'make trot'. I learn to trust my horse, Ondine, and adjust my position in harmony with her movements. She's a grey Andalusian mare, strong yet somehow elegant too. Juan says Ondine means 'water spirit', which must explain her sure-footedness as we traverse the stony riverbed. We weave our way along a river valley past poplar trees with strangely mottled bark, the clear water reflecting the lime green of the spring leaves. Ian sits confidently on Oceano, a bay horse with presence, humming the 'Bonanza' theme tune. I'm breathing in the scents of thyme and red earth after rain and gradually feeling my shoulders drop into a more relaxed pose. I pray that Juan will not consider a higher gear for the horses on this first expedition.

The day comes when we are at the bottom of a hill, looking at a rough track twisting up into a sort of Wild West canyon. The sound of the horses' hooves has echoed around us for the last five minutes, and there's an eerie silence when we stop. A bird of prey circles above us, and I glance up nervously. Juan explains that it's easiest to learn to gallop uphill the first time, as you know the horse will eventually stop. He shows us the jumping *posición* that we will need to adopt.

The horses remain completely still. We stand up on the stir-rups and lean forward, the mane in our left hand and the reins in our right. I can hear my own heartbeat, but then I remember reading how to turn the body's 'fight or flight' response into a positive asset. I swallow, breathe deeply and prepare for action. And then I don't have time to think. I see Ian disappear round the bend, Oceano's rear legs kicking up dust and stones in my face, the silver of the horseshoes glinting in the sun. I duck my head to protect myself from pebble missiles, and I'm off. And suddenly I fly with Ondine on a 'pinion of wild'. It is effortless; she is doing the work for me, and I am released from the pain of endless trotting.

I don't want it to be over, but we reach a point near the top of the canyon where Ondine runs out of steam. I pat her on the neck, falling forward in a silent prayer of thanks beneath a spreading olive tree. I don't let her eat it.

Juan is standing at the head of the pass. 'You do very well.' He grins. 'Is easy. Next time you make gallop on flat'.

On the last day in Guadix I'm sitting outside the cave, watching the mangy dog play with a piece of litter. We still haven't got rid of him, but the cave feels like home. The sun is shining on the poplars, the snow is disappearing from the mountains and I can just make out Ondine and Oceano in Juan's yard, waiting to be saddled. I realise I'm looking forward to flying on a pinion of wild. On the flat.

Music in winter

ↄ

It was mid-morning when Katja noticed the baby had gone.

The shepherds were still lined up on the left of the oak table at a respectful distance from Mary and Joseph, with the wise men on the right. Katja checked one final time behind the manger.

'Someone's taken Jesus,' she said to Darius, who was leaning against the notice board in the entrance hall of Thirlestane House. Thirlestane was Scottish Baronial; Katja was proud to work in a building with turrets and had emailed photos to her family in Krakow. Darius was tall, dark and new on the staff, and she was hopeful the conversation would lead to more than the whereabouts of the baby.

'Send oot the wise men to look for him, hen!' shouted Joe, trundling the tea trolley across the oak-panelled hall with its sweeping staircase. He made a manoeuvre to avoid Stella, who was standing by the front door, leaning on her stick. She was wearing a pleated skirt and one of the blue Pringle jumpers she favoured. Her grey hair was neatly styled, her face expressionless.

Darius and Katja enjoyed a moment of shared laughter with Joe. Stella didn't react. She was peering through the glass, trying to understand the indistinct shapes of the holly bushes in the half-light of the shortest day. She tried the handle. It was locked, because this was a prison. It wasn't opened with a key, though. They pressed those buttons on the wall. Sometimes Laura came in through that door. Laura was her daughter, or her mother. She said the name to herself and liked it.

Darius was printing carefully on the whiteboard with a thick marker pen. THURSDAY 22 DECEMBER. WEATHER – HAIL SHOWERS. ACTIVITIES – MUSIC AND MOVEMENT AND CAROL SINGING. THREE DAYS UNTIL CHRISTMAS. HAS ANYONE SEEN THE BABY JESUS?

Katja giggled. 'You can't write that! Jesus, I mean.'

Darius added 'from the nativity scene' to his last sentence. 'There are 40 suspects, you understand,' he said, running his eye down the list of residents on the wall behind him.

Katja went over to put an arm round Stella, who was trying the door handle again.

'Come on now, Stella. Joe's just taken the tea in. Laura will be here any minute.'

Stella turned to look at the girl. She was a young one, with a bright, open face. There were two metal things in each ear and one in her nose, but her eyes were kind.

'What's your name?' Stella asked.

'Oh you're just teasing me, Stella! It's me – Katja!'

'Kat – ja,' Stella said carefully. 'I'm sorry.'

Stella wanted to ask the girl why there was a tree in the hall. And then she remembered the brightly lit things in the dark time of the year; that was when the tree came into the house. The girl took her to a seat in the lounge and brought her tea.

Stella jumped, because someone was shooting at the window with white bullets. But then she saw in the dim light that it was the hard sort of snow, the angry snow. She preferred the gentle snow...

∾

The snow has been falling lightly for several hours. It is soft and dry, and Stella bends down in the half-light to look at the footprints made by her brown suede boots. She isn't going to wear these for the concert. She clutches a bag with her party shoes; her mother has put Meltonian White on them, and she is wearing her turquoise dress with the frills and ribbons under her tweed Sunday coat. The windows of the church hall cast a muted yellow light onto the snow, and through the half-open door she hears excited laughter. She smells wax polished wood mixed with a faint tinge of damp, and she can see the lights of the Christmas tree. They have a magic coloured liquid inside that bubbles and dances; it makes the tree seem alive. Her friends are chattering on the creaky, canvas chairs, and in the kitchen the tea urn is hissing beside the trays of sausage rolls and iced cakes made by the Women's Guild.

Stella stands alone on the stage and sings 'In the Bleak Mid-winter'. She hears the applause, and Mr Mackeson the music teacher comes to talk to her mother. He mentions voice training and a scholarship...

∾

'Mum?'

Stella opened her eyes and saw the lady with the dark hair and brown eyes standing by her chair. And Stella knew it was Laura, and she liked the feel of her hand. Laura was her daughter, but she wasn't small any more.

'Why have you come?'

'Why have I come? To see you, of course.'

'They clapped for a long time when I sang. Did it take you long?'

'Three hours on the train.'

'Three hours! But you live round the corner.'

'No I don't, Mum. I live in Inverness. And this is Edinburgh.'

'Inverness? Where's that?'

'Three hours north of here.'

'North? How old are you?'

'Fifty-five.'

'You'll have passed the menopause, then.'

The residents shuffled in their chairs.

'They clapped a lot at the concert. The church concert,' Stella added. She stopped for a second, twisting her fingers round the handles of her bag. 'How was school?'

'Busy. You know what it's like with all the music stuff before Christmas.'

'Am I coming to you for Christmas? '

'They think it's better if you stay here, Mum,' Laura said quickly. 'Can you hear the Christmas carol?' She glanced at the speaker on the wall.

'Who's Carol?'

'It's 'In the Bleak Midwinter'.

'Is this Carol?' Stella took a small figure from her handbag and placed it on the coffee table.

In the hall, Laura placed the baby gently back in the manger. She could hear the residents joining in with the singing, and then she stopped, because her mother's strong alto voice rose above them all. She was singing every word of 'In the Bleak Midwinter'.

There was silence, then applause.

Youth dew

ᏉᎧ

Perfume is the unseen but unforgettable and ultimate fashion accessory. It heralds a woman's arrival and prolongs her departure.

— Coco Chanel

Betty wakes, and the room doesn't smell like home. There's an underlying hint of disinfectant. The walls are pale green; it's not a colour she would have chosen. It must be seven o' clock, because there's that metallic knocking in the radiators as the heating system comes to life. Over the grey rooftops and chimneys of Edinburgh smoke hangs in the still air of an autumn morning. Betty hears the distant buzz of traffic in the world of which she's no longer a part. The armchairs by the window are the ones that were in the lounge back home in Crail. Betty's eyes linger over the painting of her favourite beach at Elie; that's where she used to walk and listen to the sea. When she turns over in bed, the weakness and tingling in her legs are still there, and she remembers again that she can't walk.

But Betty dances in her dreams. There she is, in the Cavendish Ballroom near Tollcross on a Saturday night, chattering to her friends in the cloakroom, laughing as she stands by the mirror, combing her shoulder-length dark hair. She's wearing the new red dress, the skirt made full by two stiff net petticoats. She bought it in Binns with her first wages from the bank. For a sixpence you can get a spray of scent from the machine on the wall; it's *Blue Grass* by Elizabeth Arden, and it makes her think of blue flowers that wave in the breeze. She makes her way along the draughty corridor to the dance hall. The sound of the music gets louder, and now she's in the vast room with its pillars and arches, the floor vibrating beneath her feet. Couples are crowded together, stepping out to the music of the Cavendish Dance Band. Rainbow colours from the revolving mirrored ball drift over them like confetti. As the saxophone lingers over the final notes, she sees Donald. He's walking towards her.

'Betty? Would you like a cup of tea?'

There's a gentle hand on her shoulder, and the rattle of a cup and saucer being placed on the bedside table. Betty's eyes are closed but she knows the cup is green and the tea is strong, with too much milk. It's Carrie, the young one from Stirling. That means the spoon will be on the wrong side of the saucer, and it's Saturday. Betty will read the *Scotsman*, do the crossword and sleep for an hour after lunch. She'll have the same conversation as yesterday with Ron and Elsie and George; she'll smile and pretend they don't have memory loss. And in the evening she'll watch *Strictly Come Dancing*; she'll move her hands to the music and sing along when they have the old songs like 'Moon River'. And maybe Scott will ring. He and Jane are having what they call a career break; they said it was the time to do it, now that Steph's at university. Their latest postcard of the Rockies is on the windowsill, just to the right of the one from New York. Betty would like to go there some day on the Queen Mary. She opens her eyes and reaches tentatively for the tea.

Betty hears two sets of footsteps on the corridor after mid-morning coffee. One of the people has high heels. There's chatter and laughter, and suddenly there's a perfume that Betty knows, and she sits up, her pulse quickening. It is moss, sandalwood, the warmth of the Orient.

Carrie's face appears at the door. 'Hi Betty – you've got a wee visitor today. This is Sophie.'

The girl's long blonde hair must be dyed, as her skin tone and eyes are dark. She isn't wee. She's tall, and she's smiling at Betty, evidently not intimidated by the surroundings. She's wearing thick black tights, a short denim skirt with frayed edges, and knee-length boots. Her jacket is red, and a bulky handbag is hooked over her left shoulder, distorting her frame. There are two earrings in each lobe, and she's wearing that perfume.

'Sophie's doing her Duke of Edinburgh Award. Isn't that nice? Going to be helping out from time to time – bringing you drinks, coming in for a wee chat and what have you.' Carrie's voice tails off as she heads down the corridor.

'*Youth Dew*,' Betty says.

'How did you know?' Sophie gasps. She stands with one hand on the door-frame. 'It's the first time I've worn it! My mum gets perfume samples, you see.'

The girl's accent is a surprise. It's posh Edinburgh, the marker of a good school: Watson's or Mary Erskine's, Betty guesses.

'I used it when I was your age.'

'Cool! So it's not a new one then?'

Sophie's looking at Betty's North Face fleece. Scott had got it for her at Mountain Equipment and they'd joked a bit about where her crampons were. It's comfortable with tracksuit bottoms, and the red sets off her grey hair. It's not what people expect, though.

'Tell me about yourself, dear,' Betty says, motioning to the chair beside her.

'Me? Well, I'm at Watson's – final year. Going to uni next September if I get an offer from St Andrews.'

'Ah, the home of golf.' Betty smiles. 'I used to play, you see.'

'My Dad plays golf. And we live out at Barnton,' Sophie continues. 'Me and my Mum, that is. My Dad's in the Army. He's been abroad since last April, but... we can't join him.' The girl twists her hands awkwardly, and hesitates. 'It's Afghanistan.'

'Ah, that's hard, being separated.' Betty watches Sophie play with the handles of her bag.

'I could bring you some *Youth Dew* if you like it.' The girl looks her in the eye again. 'Mum works on the Estée Lauder counter at Jenners. She got kind of bored with Dad being away...'

'Could you?' Betty is surprised at her own eagerness.

'Sure. I've decided I don't really like it myself. It's more of an old person's perfume. My favourite's *Tom Ford* – that's for Saturday nights clubbing in town.'

'Ah well, I wouldn't know about that. You'll have to tell me more next time,' says Betty.

It is not only the perfume that lingers after Sophie has gone. The girl has filled the room with an intangible liveliness, and for a moment Betty feels as if she can move the legs deadened for so long by the stroke. But as she struggles to change position in her chair she realises it's an illusion.

Sophie has filled Betty's mind with images of moving, of dancing, of lightness. And she is young again, back in the

Cavendish. Nineteen fifty-three or so, it must have been, because she'd just started work. She can see the girls lined up on one side of the room waiting for the young men to come over. And then Donald walks towards her, smiling with his eyes. That tall figure in a suit and a narrow tie, his dark hair slicked back with Brylcreem. He'd given her the *Youth Dew* for her birthday; that was it. They would dance on Saturday nights and she'd wear it for him. And on Sundays they would walk, sometimes, laughing and heading down Arthur's Seat to the Old Town and, as the light faded, on to Princes Street where she'd get the bus home.

And then there were the years after he'd gone, when she kept that perfume for Sundays, just to retain a small memory of him. It was her secret, amid all the scents that made Sunday different – fur coats and mothballs, extra strong peppermints, bread and wine and the musty dark pine of churches.

Betty sits up with a start. Carrie is drawing the curtains and switching on the table lamp. Soon Jess will come to get her ready for tea. It's high tea, and there won't be wine, but Jess will give her a glass of sherry from the cupboard in the corner before they take her down. She'll hold the crystal glass up to the light and admire the rich brown of the amontillado and enjoy its reassuring warmth in her throat. Seven more sherries, and Sophie will be back.

On weekdays Betty watches *Countdown*; her brain is still keen even if her body is packing in. It's probably better this way round. Better than John McGregor, who wanders the corridors restlessly, troubling everyone with the same questions, not knowing where his home is or who his family are.

Sophie's just made Earl Grey tea, no milk. She hands it to Betty in one of her Royal Worcester cups.

'This is quite a surprise, you coming on a Friday, dear. Now let's have a little laugh at *Countdown*. That Rachel Riley knows it all,' says Betty. 'Far too smug.'

'Her dress is too tight,' says Sophie with satisfaction. 'Which perfume do you think she uses? Oh – I forgot! I brought you some.'

It's still that deep amber, but the bottle is different; Betty fingers the ribbed glass and the gold metal bow. She sprays a little on her wrist, and inhales. The sensation is like time travel.

'A friend once gave it to me, Sophie.' Betty pauses, still cradling the bottle in her hand. 'We lost touch.'

Sophie's questioning expression forces Betty to continue. Betty isn't yet sure if she wants to talk about it; she hopes her voice will not waver too much.

'Donald. We met at the dance hall down at Tollcross. We dated for a year or so. But then he went on National Service – Germany it was. I can't remember exactly where. Anyway, I never heard from him again.'

'Oh, that's sad. Sad and romantic.' Sophie sits up in her chair and leans forward. 'Did you ever try to find him?'

'Well, I didn't. You see, I married someone else in the end. Bill was a good man, an elder of the kirk. Captain of the golf club, too. And we had our son Scott. Up on the Fife coast, that's where we lived, looking out over the sea to the Isle of May. Bill's been gone twenty years now. Cancer.' Betty turns to stare out of the window. The gardener is raking leaves on the lawn. She didn't expect to reveal so much.

'And you never thought about Donald? What's his surname?' Sophie, preferring the pursuit of a mystery to commiserating about Bill, is rummaging in the large handbag, eventually producing a slim rectangular case.

'That's an iPad, isn't it?' Betty says.

'Wow!'

'I was wondering if I could get one, actually. My legs are useless, but my hands are fine. I could be in touch with Scott and Jane with that email thing. And read their blog.'

'I could help you. And there's Skype. You can talk to people and see them with that,' says Sophie. 'But hey, what was this guy's surname?'

'Trueman. Donald Trueman.'

'That's a relief.' Sophie is already putting it into Google. 'We wouldn't have had a chance if it had been Macdonald.'

The sound of laughter echoes in the room and along the corridor.

The days are short and dark. A cold wind is blowing in from the Forth, detaching the last of the brittle leaves that cling to the silver birches. Betty can see a thin line of snow on the tops of the Pentlands and knows the Christmas season is not far off; there will be four weeks of lights and baubles and piped carols and old people's treats. Santa comes when you're under ten and over eighty. She will have to go along with it.

She turns when she hears the footsteps.

'I've brought you a perfume sample!' Sophie is out of breath and flushed from the cold air. She unwinds a thick wool scarf from round her neck. 'It's a different Estée Lauder. It's *Knowing*. What do you think?'

'It's beautiful.'

'That's another one – *Beautiful*. Then there's *Pleasures*, and the latest one is *Intuition*.'

'What marvellous names!' says Betty. 'I think I know why you brought *Knowing*. Am I right? Have you heard anything yet?'

'Not yet,' says Sophie. 'But – my Dad's coming home for Christmas! And maybe he can help.'

Betty reaches out for Sophie's hand. She sees their hands together, the young one and the old one.

'Enjoy it while he's with you. Oh, and wear *Beautiful* for him. I think that is your perfume.'

'I will. And I'll bring them to meet you, my mum and dad. Is that OK?'

It will be a better Christmas, then.

A man taps his way with a stick down the corridor of Ravelston House. He is walking awkwardly, slightly stooped, with the limp that has been his since the accident long ago in Germany. The cell-like rooms are all the same, but the girl called Sophie said that when he got to the end of the corridor he would know the room. This place reminds him of the months in hospital and the nightmares after the explosion. He's grateful he doesn't have those so often now, and that he can live with his daughter. She dropped him off at the gate this afternoon; he said he wanted to do this on his own. He hesitates as he passes each open doorway, fearful of what he may see. In some, the inhabitants lie with their eyes closed. A lady in a pink dressing gown tries to talk to him, taking his hand, asking to go home.

He stops. He can't quite say what makes the perfume distinctive. But then he remembers the counter in Jenners and choosing it for a girl in a red dress. He remembers the closeness of her, and he remembers her smile as they turn together on the dance floor, oblivious to the others. She is light on her feet, light in her smile, light in her heart.

Youth… Youth Dew… Rich, warm and oriental. That was it. He knows this is the room.

He knocks gently, and pushes the half-open door, his hand shaking. The lady in the wheelchair turns round and smiles at him.

'May I have the pleasure?' he says.

Castles in the air

❧

Schwerin floats on water, surrounded by seven lakes. The city is only sixty miles east of Hamburg, but for a generation that route was blocked by the mines and trip wires of the 'death strip', the border separating East and West Germany. As a legacy of those years, my journey to Schwerin was circuitous. The Inter City express from Hamburg moved softly north east towards the red spires of Lübeck on the Baltic coast, passing neat houses with criss-cross wooden fences and gardens alive with geraniums. At Lübeck, I crossed the divide without a visa, changing on to a train that creaked its way south east, forbidden to travel faster than a hundred kilometres per hour on the aging tracks. Then at Bad Kleinen, a down-at-heel junction in shades of brown, I sat alone on the platform awaiting the Schwerin train, almost tasting the rust, slowly taking in the peeling paint and the weeds on the station roof.

It is August, 1990. I've travelled through the looking glass to the 'other Germany'. And now I'm looking at a castle on a hexagonal island, its towers and cupolas pointing to a cloudless sky. Behind its dark brown walls, the lake shimmers blue-grey in the heat. At any minute I expect to see Rapunzel confirm I'm in a fairytale by opening the window to let down her hair. Next to me, an old lady dressed in black squints in the afternoon sun, taking in the view. She leans on a stick, grey hair tied back in a bun.

'Ist doch schön,' she says, lingering on the long vowel of *schön*. I nod in agreement.

'So ein schönes Gerüst!' she adds.

I hesitate before agreeing, because it's not what I expect to hear: she's admiring the scaffolding. She's lived with the acrid smell of brown coal and buildings darkened by pollution. But suddenly Schwerin castle has changed; the new metal of West German scaffolding sparkles in the sun, and we jump as a drill roars into action. The sign says a West German company is doing renovation work. Should I say 'West German' now? It's difficult to know. It is nine months since the Berlin Wall fell, and Helmut Kohl is on his way to becoming Chancellor of a Germany that will be united in October. We've just had the currency reform, and further along the road unfamiliar Deutschmarks are being exchanged for Coca Cola.

The old lady is Oma, grandmother. She lives with her son Kurt Eggert, his wife Dora, and their two children Lisa and Tobi, and they're showing me Schwerin. Tobi, with dark hair and dark brown eyes, tugs at his mother's hand. He's already told me he's five and will soon go to school. Lisa is seven. She comes running towards us, brown hair flying, pointing at the kiosk.

'Look! Langnese ice cream. I've never had that one before.'

The man who serves us doesn't look us in the eye as he drops the change down on the counter.

My friend Karin in Hamburg suggested this trip.

'I'd like you to go,' she said. 'You need to see how easy it is now, just to cross over. I have a cousin in Schwerin, you know.'

Karin liked me to experience history 'live'. Over the years I'd been fascinated and saddened by the tales of her family, divided for so many years by the Wall. The last time she had sent me east was in 1972, to Berlin. I had stood for hours on a crowded train, waiting for the border guards at Helmstedt to scrutinise the transit visas. They gave us no greeting. With other tourists in Berlin I had dutifully photographed the Wall and the concrete watchtowers, just making out the shapes of the guards poised to shoot anyone attempting to escape. It had felt unreal, as if I was on a film set.

My arrival in Schwerin twenty-four hours previously had seemed unreal too. I see myself standing in the bare station foyer, its cracked plaster walls painted a dirty shade of beige. I can't help thinking I'm being watched, that my clothes mark me as western. I remember reading that a surprisingly large percentage of East Germans were employed by the STASI and that many ordinary citizens were 'inoffizielle Mitarbeiter', unofficial 'helpers', informing on friends and even family. I wonder how many of them are here in the station, buying West German papers like *Die Welt* or *Frankfurter Allgemeine* with Deutschmarks. I wonder what I'll do if Kurt doesn't come, and I fleetingly scan the departures board for the time of the next train back to Hamburg. I notice that some people's skins have an unhealthy, almost translucent pallor. The clothes are plainer, simpler, monotonous in their colouring, with more than a hint of synthetic material. There's a lot of beige, and a lot of dark blue. The cigarette smoke in the air smells alien, as if it doesn't come from tobacco. I'm thinking about moving outside when Kurt finds me in the crowd.

Kurt is in his early forties, slim with short dark hair, a well-trimmed beard and bright eyes. He's wearing a checked jacket and jeans. We shake hands, and converse in German. He doesn't speak English; like everyone else in the German Democratic Republic he learned Russian at school. We stroll past parked Trabants and cross a cobbled square in front of the station, heading for his home in Karl Marx Allee. Kurt explains that very little of Schwerin was destroyed in the war. Behind the dirty grey veneer, some of the architecture is inspiring; the buildings, often with carved gable ends facing the streets, have symmetry and elegance.

The Eggerts' home faces a tree-rimmed lake, the Pfaffenteich. It's what the Germans call an Altbauwohnung – a flat in an old property with high ceilings, big windows, and polished parquet floors. We turn into the living room, gloomy with dark oak furniture. Through a half-open connecting door, a thin voice calls out 'Willkommen!' from behind a disarray of bookcases, wardrobes, ornaments and suitcases. These are Oma's rooms, filled with eighty years' worth of possessions.

Kurt's wife Dora welcomes me warmly. She's just returned from her morning shift at the hospital and is cooking lunch, still wearing her white nurse's uniform. She runs a hand through her dark hair as if she is always in a rush. The two children are doing a jigsaw on the floor.

'Sie kommt aus dem Westen, aus England,'* Dora tells Lisa.

---

* *She comes from the West, from England.*

'Aber sie spricht Deutsch.'* Lisa looks up, puzzled.

I explain that I've spent years learning German. We get out an atlas and I put a finger on my hometown.

'You had to cross blue to get here,' Tobi says. 'Wow!'

'Yes, I crossed blue.'

'I've never crossed blue,' he says. 'Well, only the lake.'

He is wearing a T-shirt with a cartoon picture of a plane and the words 'Flughafen Köln Bonn'.

'I'm sure you'll go some day,' I say.

'When I get a new car we'll drive west, ' says Kurt.

'Maybe you'll come to England, then.'

The atlas is left out on the table while we have lunch: meatballs, rice, and a salad of organic garden lettuce and cucumber. We drink apple juice from a local co-operative; people take apples there from their gardens and return to claim free juice.

'You see, we have some good ideas in the East,' Kurt says, pouring out the juice. 'I don't know what will happen to the co-operative now, whether it will continue in its present form. It's such a strange time for us. We can't believe what's happened and the speed of it. It wasn't even called a revolution. It was *die Wende*, the turning point.'

'We're thrilled to be free, yet we're apprehensive. It's a sort of limbo time,' Dora adds. She stands up to clear the table, turning to the children, who are beginning to yawn. 'Maybe we'll go out in the car this afternoon. How about the Pinnower See?'

There are cries of enthusiasm as the children run for swimming costumes and towels.

---

* *But she speaks German.*

The Eggerts' car is a Wartburg, the more upmarket of the two brands available in the German Democratic Republic. As we move out from the centre of Schwerin, we pass terraces of dull brick and the prefabricated, concrete blocks of flats of a suburb called Großer Dreesch. The car rattles and bounces along a cobbled road that is patched and uneven. Soon we're out in the country, passing houses with vegetable patches and hens pecking at the dusty ground.

Dora asks me about my job and I tell her I teach languages.

'I'd love to have been a teacher,' she says. 'The State wouldn't allow it. My father was a priest, you see, and that meant no Abitur*, no university. I love nursing, but it wasn't my first choice.'

It's hard to take in this lack of personal freedom.

'Kurt works in admin,' she continues. 'It isn't a great job, because he wasn't a Party member, but he never wanted to be a Party member. He's not sure what will happen in his office now. Everything's in upheaval. He'd really like to start his own business, if he can. We'll just have to wait and see.'

I realise she may be telling me this in the car out of habit. You can't be overheard here.

'Was there pressure put on you? To join the Party, I mean?' I ask Kurt.

'For a while. Then they gave up.' He keeps his eyes on the road. 'But you knew you were on the list then, being watched.'

There is silence, and we turn our minds to the pleasures of the present. Kurt slows the car and pulls into a car park.

---

* The German equivalent of A-levels.

We walk to a grassy area by the lakeshore, sheltered by willows which blow in the light breeze. Families are out enjoying the late afternoon sun, chatting and laughing. There's an aroma of barbecued sausages, and I hear the dull thud of footballs and the jingle of beer crates being carried from cars. Away from the town, it seems like anywhere else in Germany. Shafts of light filter through the silver birch trees as we walk towards the water. And nobody is watching.

The water is surprisingly warm. I swim towards Tobi and Kurt, feeling more relaxed in my new environment.

'It's a beautiful world, Dad, isn't it?' Tobi smiles. He says it lightly, innocently. His father smiles too. He gathers Tobi up in his arms and carries him to the shore.

On my last day, I linger in the city centre. I pass shop windows with meagre displays, but there are also some splashes of colour which announce that West German firms have moved in. A yellow sign for a summer sale lights up the front of a drab fashion store. Ladies grab at the bright clothes and study the price tags.

I take a seat at a nearby pavement café. I'm surprised to see so many Soviet soldiers. Since *die Wende* it seems there's nowhere for them to go back home to and they, like the East Germans, are in limbo. Some have quickly absorbed the spirit of enterprise and are selling their uniforms on the streets as souvenirs, making enough for a few beers. The variations in their facial features make me aware of the extent of the USSR and its empire, stretching east to Vladivostok, to the Pacific. But whether they're from Estonia, Armenia, Georgia or Kamchatka, they are now relaxing.

They even smile for the cameras of the Americans, Japanese and West Germans who have come to look at the country that has been locked up for so long.

The sound of violins dances in the air; two girls are playing by the cathedral. As is often the case in Germany, it's classical busking by students from one of the many Musikschulen. The music of the Bach double violin concerto silences the crowd as the voices of the instruments intertwine. In the hat on the pavement the new money glints in the sun. We clap when they draw to a close. And when our applause stops, we hear the distant hammering of construction work.

Before I leave, Oma presents me with a postcard. It's a large one on thin card, featuring the main sights of Schwerin in distorted colours – the castle, the cathedral, the opera house and two holiday homes of the Free German Trade Union Federation.

'I looked a long time for a nice one,' she says, taking my hand.

Oma died three months later, on the ninth of November, one year exactly after the fall of the Berlin Wall. She lived the last month of her life in a united Germany.

❧

It is August 1995, and I'm at home when the phone rings.

'I'm crossing blue! We're coming!' Tobi is the first to speak.

His father takes the phone from him.

'I can see white cliffs,' Kurt says. 'And I never thought I'd leave Germany. Ever.' His voice trembles.

Kurt has his own mobile phone firm; he has hit on an ideal

product at an ideal time, and business is booming. He's bought a mobile phone before I have, and the Wartburg has been exchanged for a second-hand Passat. He uses his mobile phone enthusiastically on the journey north, calling me whenever an interpreter is required. I talk to the owner of a Surrey campsite, the driver of a London sightseeing bus, and a custodian at Warwick Castle.

In our garden, we drink tea and talk of changed lives. They've brought us a book of aerial photos of Schwerin. The book is printed in Bremen; the colours sparkle on the page, clear and true.

'Oh look, here's your house! And the lake. And the castle – there's still scaffolding on two of the towers.' I leaf through it, looking for familiar sights.

'That's where our story began,' says Kurt.

Dora turns to me. She looks happy, more relaxed. 'I'd like to see the sea,' she says. 'You know we love to swim. We're not so far from the coast here, are we?'

I explain about the quicksands of Morecambe Bay, and her face falls. 'But there's a walk we could do. We could climb a hill and you'd see the sea, and the Lake District mountains.'

'It's the sea I want to look at.' she says. 'The Atlantic.'

We stand on Arnside Knott, facing Morecambe Bay. The children are at the view indicator, their fingers tracing out the line of the hills.

'Ist doch schön!' Kurt says. 'Der Atlantik.'

Dora nods in agreement. She stands in the sun, taking in the panorama.

'I'd like to cross the Atlantic some day. Go to America,' says Lisa.

'Me too,' says Tobi.

Part of me wants to speak the truth, because I know they were once denied it. But sometimes a fairy tale is better. It's the notion of looking west that's important, even if it's really the Irish Sea.

'You will cross the Atlantic,' I say. 'Live your dreams.'

Epilogue 2015

The scars of the 'death strip' are no longer visible. Schwerin sparkles with renovated buildings, and there are few reminders of German Democratic Republic days. Karl Marx Allee has been renamed Alexandrinenstraße. The castle is now the State Parliament of Mecklenburg-Vorpommern.

I was Kurt and Dora's first visitor from the West. They have continued to welcome others into their home, including exchange students from Mexico and Estonia. Lisa and Tobi have travelled as far afield as Mexico, Alaska and Uzbekistan, and speak several languages.

Road to joy

လာ

On 9th November, 2014 thousands of white balloons were released into the sky to commemorate the fall of the Berlin Wall in 1989.

Johann holds my hand. The final members of the audience move to their seats. And then the primeval call of the oboe rises above the chatter. I look up, goosebumps dancing on my neck. It's that sense of anticipation, of something about to be born. Like a lone bird it soars above the other instruments, leading the way. And it is Anna who is playing.

'*Das ist Mama!* Cool! Hey, your palm's sweaty.' Johann looks up at me.

'It's a special sound. The oboe.'

'It's like a duck, Papa. And you hear it all the time at home, when Mama's practising. So it's not special.'

'They say it's the instrument most like the human voice, Johann. There's something sad about it. But it can be happy too,' I add quickly.

'So, why does Mama get to start, then?'

'Well, it's not the proper piece. The orchestra is tuning up. Making sure all the instruments play together on the right notes. Mama plays an A, and they all follow.' I can't go too much into the physics of it. He's only six.

'So what's the proper piece?'

'The proper piece... the tune... is by someone called

Beethoven. It's called Ode to Joy.'

'What's an ode, Papa?'

'It's a kind of poem. Schiller, the poet who wrote it, was just saying how he felt about something. How he felt about joy.'

'What's joy?'

'Well, it's being very, very happy. It doesn't always last a long time but you know it when you feel it.'

'Like Christmas?'

'Yes! Like a wonderful, wonderful present. Joy is seeing Mama there, playing.'

'Like the line of white balloons we saw on the way here!' he says. 'Flying up into the sky. I don't believe the Berlin Wall was there, Papa. There are those bits at the East Side Gallery. But mostly it's not there, is it?'

'I saw it, Johann. I saw it come down. And we came to a concert back then, right here in the Philharmonie. With your mama, and her family. We were sitting over there.' I point to where the balcony overhangs the stage. The orchestra members sit like black statues, awaiting the arrival of Sir Simon Rattle. 'The concert was a special treat. For us, from the East. It was a different conductor, though. Daniel Barenboim. He's the conductor who's playing at the Brandenburg Gate tonight with the Staatskapelle.'

'I'd rather be here in the warm, watching Mama.'

'*Ja, gut,* Anna! But I think you know it's not as good as it could be.' Frau Schultmann, oboe teacher at the Hanover *Musikschule*, pursed her lips. 'It's only a week till the Youth Orchestra concert, you know.'

Anna looked through the *Musikschule* window at the November rain. The wind was blowing the last, brittle leaves from the chestnut trees by the Maschsee.

'I know, Frau Schultmann. Somehow, with the news and everything… life just hasn't been normal this week.'

'Ach! So exciting! So unbelievable! But promise me—'

'You know I'll do it. Next week it will be perfect.'

All the way home in the tram to Kleefeld, the chatter was of Berlin and this most startling news of her lifetime. But Anna thought about the concert. It had to be her best; each concert was a step on the way to a *Konservatorium* place.

The *Tagesschau* was blaring out in the sitting room, and Mama was translating the news commentary for Gran, who was over from Scotland. Mama was Scottish; she'd met Papa at university in Heidelberg. The joy in the television pictures didn't need a translator; the crowds were alive, dancing and singing by the Brandenburg Gate.

Anna took off her coat.

'We've go to go Anna! It's such an opportunity,' Mama said. 'And with Gran here … think what she'll say to her friends when she goes home! We can stay with Horst and Martina. I've rung them and it's fine. Join the party, they said.'

'But, Mama! It's the concert next week and— ' Anna fought the urge to bite her nails.

'Don't be saying you can't afford the time. This is history, girl! And anyway, you're too much of a perfectionist.' Papa sat back, sipping his evening beer. The froth stuck to his moustache. 'You'll be fine.'

After *Abendbrot,* Mama wrapped up the cheeses and cold meats and replaced them in the plastic boxes. She was unusually quiet.

'Such an easy way to have supper, here!' Gran broke the silence. 'I think I might start doing this when I get home to Kirkcaldy.' She took the boxes over to the fridge. 'Now, Berlin...' She turned to Anna. 'Go on! I want a wee piece of the Berlin Wall. Take your oboe with you.'

Anna's hand touched the oboe case on the back seat of the Passat. It had been two hours since they had joined the steady procession of Volkswagens and Audis eager to be part of history. Trabants drove in the opposite direction; the drivers tooted and waved, miraculously released to explore what had once been forbidden territory.

'Will you take a look at these cars!' Gran exclaimed. 'They look like they were made fifty years ago!'

'I think they're cute, actually.' Anna leaned out to wave, then closed the window as rough petrol fumes caught the back of her throat.

At the border crossing point at Helmstedt, the officials didn't look official any more. Some of them were actually smiling. And that was the moment when Anna first felt a tingling sensation that her life might change.

'So will there be two Germanies, or just one?'

'I have no idea, Anna. That's the exciting part.' Mama had the road atlas out and was checking the way to Horst's house in Wannsee.

'So if there's going to be just one Germany, Hanover wouldn't be in the east of West Germany, it would be in the centre.' Anna tried to comprehend the strangeness of this. For the fourteen years of her life there had been a barrier to the East that you couldn't cross without lengthy dealings with state authorities. And you knew that, even if you got the paperwork, you would be scrutinised by the *Stasi* all the time you were over there.

Gran had fallen asleep despite the bumpy road surface. The motorway seemed to be paved in cobbles. It was dark now, and they couldn't see anything beyond the wire fences at the side of the motorway. Jolting over a series of potholes, they were drawn steadily towards the orange glow of Berlin in the eastern sky.

Anna took her oboe out of its case and fingered the rising and descending scales of the Beethoven piece.

Johann is leaning over the balcony rail.

'Mama isn't playing all the time,' he whispers. 'Did she forget a bit?'

'She would never do that.' I smile. 'No, they don't all play all the time. They each get their turn. And when they're not playing they have to count. And make sure they come in at the right time again.'

'That's hard.'

'But you listen and watch. There will come a time when they all play together.'

'I'm watching the drums, now,' Johann says. 'Boom, boom!'

They heard the Wall before they saw it. It was late evening, yet it was as crowded as Kröpke on the Saturday before Christmas. People were dancing to a rock band, drinking *Sekt* and singing, but over all that came a persistent tapping like a thousand woodpeckers in a fairytale forest. It was the sound of hammers on concrete. Gran moved forward eagerly.

The collapsed, graffitied panels lay like a broken-up jigsaw. Anna had been at the Wall once before, on a school trip. That was when she had realised it was serious, because there were mines and barbed wire and East German soldiers who had orders to shoot anyone that crossed. They'd been told all about the history but it seemed as if it had nothing to do with her; it had to do with the War, and what happened after. Now, as she touched the place where the dividing line had been, she felt different.

Spicy aromas of Glühwein and grilled sausages drifted over from a nearby stall, bringing Anna back to the present. She turned to ask the others if they'd like something, and then suddenly she couldn't see Mama, or Papa. Or Gran, or her hammer. She began to panic as she felt the crush and push of the crowd. Between jostling heads and bulky shoulders she could just make out two policemen in different uniforms, one from the East and one from the West, chatting and laughing. And as she wondered which one might help her, the crowd convulsed together in one huge wave. She stumbled onto the pavement, and lay there, covering her head in her hands.

'Wow! That choir is huge.'

Johann is pretending to conduct, and I don't stop him. He has a sense of rhythm. 'How many singers are there? Can we count them? Oh… and Mama's playing!'

I put my finger to my lips. He quietens down, and the great

hall of the Philharmonie reverberates as 'Ode to Joy' works up to its climax. The choir sings of freedom and brotherhood, Sir Simon Rattle dances on the podium, and every member of the orchestra plays.

'You all right?'

A man and a woman, both dressed in denim jackets, towered over Anna. The teenage boy behind them looked about Anna's age.

'I lost my family…'

'Your family? From West Berlin?'

She shook her head. 'From Hanover. We came to visit some friends, see what's going on…'

'Anna! Anna!'

Mama and Papa were pushing their way through the crowd. Gran lurched to one side, weighed down by her handbag.

'I've never met anyone from Hanover,' the man said. 'I've never been on this side before.'

There was one moment of silence beneath the November stars. The band had stopped. Anna could see the condensation from the man's breath suspended in the air. Papa helped her up.

The boy was looking at her, eyes wide. 'We just walked over Bornholmer Straße… and here we are!'

Anna smiled, but words wouldn't come.

'It's a miracle! I can't believe…' The woman nodded and beamed. She glanced down at her feet, firmly planted on Western soil. Her skin was pale, almost translucent, but her eyes shone.

The man hesitated. 'Would you … would you like to visit us?

I know we are strangers, but it would be an honour to have our first visitors from the West. I am Markus.'

They shook hands. His wife was Herta, his son Matthias.

That was how they came to stand in the draughty stairwell of the concrete block of flats in East Berlin, outside the door with the nameplate 'Müller'. It was the commonest name in West Germany; Anna smiled to think there were Müllers in the East too.

The applause goes on for a good three minutes. The audience is upstanding and cries of 'bravo!' ring in the air. Johann is leaning over the balcony rail, waving to Anna. She's looking up at him.

'*Fantastisch*, Mama!'

'It's not just her show, Johann.'

He starts to move towards the aisle. 'Can we go to the Sony Center after this?'

'Well, maybe. It's well after your bedtime though.'

'Papa. You and Mama. Tell me that story again.'

'You know the story, Johann.'

'So you took Mama's family to that concert. With that Baron guy.'

'Barenboim. Daniel Barenboim.'

'Was that concert better?'

'They were both the best concerts I've ever been to Johann.'

'They can't both be best. I thought only one thing could be best.'

'They were both pretty special.'

He looks up at me. We're in the foyer now, and Anna is there, calling to us.

'Matthias! Johann!'

Johann runs to her. *'Mama, es war perfekt!'*

And as we walk out into the crisp night air we see the last of the white balloons rising up into the night sky.

The story behind the stories

The stories in this collection are a product of my three years of Creative Writing with the Open University, during which I studied short fiction, poetry, life writing, drama and script-writing. 'Music in winter' and 'Youth dew' were my earliest pieces: my experiences of saying goodbye to elderly relatives and friends were still being processed and I wanted to highlight the stories of those who sit in care home chairs and consider whether life for them was only about the past and present. The prompt for 'Music in winter' was a Facebook post by The Elms care home in Edinburgh that Jesus was missing from their nativity scene. A visit to another elderly friend who used the perfume 'Youth dew' prompted my second story. Both of these stories contain surprising changes and small messages of hope.

'Pinion of wild' and 'Castles in the air' are travel writing from my own experience. By this stage in my writing I had begun to examine intense moments of shift or change. The Spanish riding course is possibly the bravest thing I have done! My trip to Schwerin in 1990 was the time in my life where I felt truly at a turning point in history, and the image of Oma at the castle admiring the sparkling scaffolding is one that has always stayed with me. Welcoming the Eggert family to England was also very special. I returned to this period of history for the final story in my collection, 'Road to joy'. I have had strong connections with Germany over the years and felt moved to write the story on the 25th anniversary of the fall of the Berlin Wall; this story is for all my German friends.

I wrote 'Shifting sands' on the third year of my course, and was surprised and delighted when it won third prize in the Mslexia Women's Short Story Competition, 2014.

How do you write a good short story? One thing is certain; it can't be done in one evening. Jane Rogers, who judged the *Mslexia* competition, remarked that 'it can take a very long time, sometimes years, to get a literary short story right.' There were many drafts of 'Shifting sands'; it took about two months to polish in its final stages, but some of the ideas had been in my head for much longer.

I like a strong, vivid setting and I have found that I am naturally drawn to the islands of the Outer Hebrides, which I visit regularly on holiday. There is an other-worldliness about the open spaces, the empty beaches, the unpredictable weather, the colours and the quality of light. There is a strong link between character and place here, as well as a tradition of folk tales and legends. In the summer before I began to write this story, we spent a week in Howmore, South Uist, in a holiday cottage which was the former home of a Gaelic bard Donald John Macdonald, whose father Duncan MacDonald was a well-known *seanchaidh* (storyteller). Perhaps some of the magic rubbed off!

The original opening of 'Shifting sands' was written in

response to a simple prompt about a body lying across the door-step of a church and the sound of a baby's cry. I had to continue the story using the title 'Woman in the wind'. Straight away I found myself back in South Uist. I could visualise the church of Howmore and the flowers on the machair, and I could hear the sea. When Donald led me into the blackhouse I could describe it with no difficulty. I had no idea at that stage where the story would go, or who the girl was. Later, we were asked to write a piece involving the tension of a narrow escape from an accident. I had read about the horse and trap crossing the South Ford from Benbecula to South Uist in Christina Hall's *Tales from an Island*. I decided to write about an accident here and build this into my story. The characters Catriona and Angus had appeared in the rough notes of a 'free-write' three years previously. I am not sure myself who Eilidh is, but I may have been influenced by folk tales of silkies.

I wanted the story to have a lyrical quality and drafted it initially as a narrative poem with verses told alternately from the points of view of Donald, Catriona and Morag. This helped me create six sections and achieve a sense of shape and proportion. My shifting viewpoint characters became like the shifting sands and shifting truth. I also wanted the story to have a timeless feel. It is clearly not modern, but the age is not specified. As regards the language, I knew my characters would be Gaelic speakers, and I had to convey that somehow through a lilting tone in the English and some attention to the vocabulary and word order.

An invitation to provide a German version of 'Shifting sands' for the German anthology *Weibsbilder*, edited by Gabriele Haefs and Karin Braun, was an exciting development. 'Treibsand' was published in *Weibsbilder* by Edition Narrenflug, Kiel, in 2015.

In the final year of my studies we considered links between drama and fiction writing. 'Cross words', an amalgamation of my retired friends' experiences, was originally written as a short stage play, and 'Ships that pass' was a radio play. Studying drama has strongly influenced my subsequent writing, helping me to see the action, consider cut scenes and hear the characters' voices.

Some family diaries and notebooks found in an attic gave me the prompt for 'Ships that pass'. Mary wrote a diary for three months, giving me an insight into life in Edwardian Glasgow in its heyday of Empire, with women on the cusp of liberation. My source material gave me the names of many of the characters and detail about everyday life – the list of wedding presents, the Sunday teaching at the Mission, the meeting of friends at Miss Cranston's Tea Rooms, Isa and her lucky farthing, Mama and her darning, the maid who leaves to get married, the regular delivery of postcards with messages from friends, the social evenings at home and Mary's singing lessons. However, the diaries did not give me a plot. One further notebook described a holiday in Melrose where Mary met some Americans who 'hustled' and were keen to see all the sights. They sounded so modern that I decided to build them into my story, along with one or two facts that I knew about Mary's subsequent life. The Americans bring views which Mary seeks in her desire to escape deep-seated Victorian values and Church traditions.

Visits to Mary's house in Craigpark, Dennistoun and to the

Glasgow museums, particularly the Riverside Museum with its trams and street reconstruction, were an enjoyable part of my research process.

Writing 'Ships that pass' as a radio play enabled me to include a bigger story than I could contain in a conventional short story of around 2,500 words. I could dart easily from scene to scene, and there was no need for lengthy descriptive passages. Above all, however, I could hear the voices and the different accents. My characters became more and more real to me.

When the course finished, I had aims to develop 'Ships that pass' as a novel, but I knew I needed much more for my plot to realise this. A request from Edition Narrenflug for a 'long story' in German was the catalyst for further work on it. I was reminded from my German studies that Theodor Storm considered the Novelle 'the sister of drama', and the 'long story' seemed right for the story I had to tell. I developed it with the framework story, another feature of the German Novelle. The German version will be published in 2016.

The stories in my collection have all shifted and changed. I present them as they were in October 2015.

Acknowledgements

I didn't do it on my own. A huge part of the pleasure is the people that have shared my journey. Special thanks go to:

My parents for instilling in me a love of language and stories;

My husband Iain for the cover photograph and his patience while I write;

David Fraser for help with my website;

Open University tutors Lucy Yates, Andrew Garvin and Nicky Harlow for their wisdom and encouragement;

OU students who helped with comments and feedback – Kath Breen, Cathy Burdett, Sue Manning, Rosie Mowatt, Shirley Osborn, Helena Sanderson, Brian Stewart, Moira Taylor, Maybelle Wallis and Lisbeth Ware;

Mslexia and Jane Rogers for permission to quote from the June/July/August 2014 edition of the magazine;

The Cochrane family for permission to use Mary's diaries as an inspiration for 'Ships that pass';

Ink Pantry Publishing, who first published 'Youth dew' in their anthology *Fields of Words*;

The Elms Care Home in Edinburgh;

Vera Thirsk, who inspired 'Youth dew';

Christine Fraser, for information on Edinburgh dance halls;

Karin Ammer and the Eggert family in Schwerin;

Jane Klatt, for her account of the fall of the Berlin Wall;

Marion Macfarlane, Mari Ottridge, Barbara Shore and Judy Wheeler who have encouraged me every step of the way;

Hilary K. Brown and Gabriele Haefs who opened up the world of publication in Germany;

Duncan at Lumphanan Press for his helpful advice about the publication process.